Slowly his eyes met hers.

"I'll come back."

His words sounded more like a torturous concession than the pleasure he normally showed for her treats. And she'd been up two hours early this morning to make them for him. *Vell*, maybe not just for him. She did have a reason.

Martin was waiting for her reply. She tried to smile over her disappointment. "Just don't take as long to come back as the last time you made that promise. My cinnamon buns won't last three years."

Understanding dawned in his expression. His somber look changed to a smile. "Don't worry, Cass. Your special recipe is as irresistible as ever."

Cass—his friendly shortened version of her name—sparked some hope in her heart.

Martin was still her friend, and he'd help her. She only had to get him to stay in Promise long enough to do so. The plate of cinnamon buns weighed heavily on her hand. They may have lost some of their usual instant charm on him, but she wasn't giving up yet.

Amy Grochowski's deep appreciation for the Amish faith and way of life stems from six years of living and working with a Beachy Amish family, as well as her own Anabaptist roots. After a nursing career of over twenty years, Amy is now fulfilling her long-awaited dream career as an author of inspirational romance. She is also a full-time homeschool mom for her two sons, one of whom has autism spectrum disorder. She lives with her family in the bustling foothills of North Carolina. Learn more at amygrochowski.com.

Books by Amy Grochowski

Love Inspired

The Amish Nanny's Promise
The Amish Baker's Secret Courtship

Visit the Author Profile page at LoveInspired.com.

The Amish Baker's Secret Courtship

AMY GROCHOWSKI

LOVE INSPIRED
INSPIRATIONAL ROMANCE

LOVE INSPIRED®

INSPIRATIONAL ROMANCE

Recycling programs
for this product may
not exist in your area.

ISBN-13: 978-1-335-59727-4

The Amish Baker's Secret Courtship

Love Inspired
22 Adelaide St. West, 41st Floor
Toronto, Ontario M5H 4E3, Canada
www.LoveInspired.com

Printed in Lithuania

MIX
Paper | Supporting
responsible forestry
FSC® C021394

Ye are of God, little children, and have overcome
them: because greater is he that is in you,
than he that is in the world.
—*1 John* 4:4

For my two sons, Nathaniel and Timothy.
You continue to inspire me with your courage,
compassion and faith beyond your years.
May you always remain such beautiful
beacons of light and overcoming through
life's difficulties and in its joys.
I love you, my brave knights.

Chapter One

Cassie Weaver plunged her fists deep into the bread dough until her knuckles disappeared into the center of the deflating pillow of yeasty softness. She wasn't always so forceful with this step of bread making—a task she performed multiple times daily on most days of the week.

Nay, the chore wasn't the source of her irritation this morning, despite how she channeled her frustration into it. In fact, she loved baking and her job in her uncle's Amish store. And Uncle Nick understood—encouraged even—her desire to open her own Amish bake shop. But her *datt*...

"*Ach!*" She dumped the dough out of the proofing container and onto the countertop, where she'd divide it into portions for loaves. "Why can't he see what a *wunnerbar goot* opportunity this is? He's never been this way before. So...so..."

"Careful, *dochter*."

Cassie jumped at the sound of her *datt*'s voice behind her. She thought she was all alone in the cooking area of the store's deli.

Tall and lanky, straw hat in his hand and his salty-gray hair parted by the same cowlick she'd inherited from him, Eli Weaver stood half grinning at her with a twinkle in his eye.

"Obstinate. Stubborn. Do either of those words work?"

He sighed. And Cassie didn't dare reply, although both words would have worked. "I'm not opposed to you starting your own business. I believe you'd do a great job at it. Just not in your uncle's farmhouse."

"Uncle Nick's farmhouse is standing empty. He and Fern and their *kinner* are happy in their new house above the store. I'm sure they wouldn't offer if it was an imposition."

Her father stepped closer and placed his hand on her arm with a gentle touch, much in the way he'd soothe an unsettled horse. "I'm not comfortable having you working alone on that large farm off the main road. Even in a small mountain town like Promise, there are dangers for a young woman alone."

"But there isn't anywhere else for the bakery."

"Cassie, let's not go through it all again. I know you disagree, but I'm your *vader*. It's my job to keep you safe. And I'm sure we can find a solution in the end that suits everyone. There's no rush, is there?"

She shook her head. "*Nay*, but I don't want to wait forever, *Datt*."

"Forever is so short to the young." He chuckled, sounding every bit the Amish minister he'd become when she was a young girl. "I won't make you wait that long before we come up with a satisfactory resolution. Give it some time to see what else might work out. That's all I ask."

She didn't want to wait, especially knowing there wasn't any other building available, not with a ready-made kitchen to start a bakery. Main Street stretched no farther than five blinks by horse and one by car along the Virginia state road leading up to the Blue Ridge Parkway. Weaver's Amish Store was the chief attraction, second only to Burkholder's Hardware and Nicely's gas station. She had high hopes of adding her own bakery to that list of Promise stores for tourists, but all the other buildings were residential and occupied.

Nay, there were no other options.

But she respected her *datt*'s wisdom. He'd never given her a reason not to trust him before. Besides, she couldn't just leave Uncle Nick in the lurch at the store. He needed to find a replacement. Hopefully by then, her *datt* would reach the same conclusion she had.

"*Ya, Datt*. That seems fair."

"*Goot*." He gave her elbow a gentle squeeze and dropped his hand.

"But *Datt*… I just wonder, why now? You hadn't said anything against this idea before last night."

He placed his hat back on his head, then spoke in a near whisper. "I think you know."

Only she didn't. She knew he had this sudden concern for her safety, but none of the ideas she came up with to remedy the issue had been enough to convince him. She'd spent most of the night and all morning trying to figure it out. It was as if everyone was privy to some secret, everyone but her. *Ach*, but her head ached from it all.

She rubbed at her temples and pulled in a deep breath.

He offered a sympathetic smile. "It's not so bad, just a bump in the road."

A bump that felt more like a mountain.

The familiar swish of the staff door opening shifted Cassie's attention from her *datt*. Fern Beiler—*nay*, Fern Weaver now, Uncle Nick's new wife—came through the entryway bearing a steaming cup of *kaffi* in her hand.

Fern smiled at them both. "*Goot mariye*, Eli. I didn't realize you were here." She held the mug out to Cassie. "Nick said you could use this."

"*Denki*, Fern." She gladly accepted the caffeinated drink,

even though she usually preferred tea. This morning, she could use the extra boost.

"How about you, Eli? I can get you a cup, too, if you'd like."

"*Nay.* No need to bother. I have to get going. But *denki* for taking care of my girl." He smiled at them both before slipping out the same way Fern had come in a moment before.

After Cassie's *datt* left, Fern raised an eyebrow. "Nick mentioned you appeared tired this morning and maybe a mite discouraged."

Fern wasn't necessarily tall. But, like almost everyone else in the world, she was taller than Cassie, who'd inherited her short stature from her *mamm* rather than her father's height. At that moment, though, Fern leaned back against the counter and slumped down a few inches to stand shoulder to shoulder with Cassie.

Fern placed a hand on her abdomen in which a new life was growing large enough to spring into the world any day.

"What is it?" Cassie's concern grew as the woman hesitated to answer. "Is it the baby?"

"*Nay.* The *boppli* is fine." Fern patted her belly.

She'd known Fern all her life. Of course, because they were both Amish in a tiny community, but also because she was Martin Beiler's older sister. A sudden panic struck at the thought of Martin. Cassie flipped around to face Fern directly. "It's not Martin, is it? Is everything alright?"

"I think maybe Eli's change of heart is *all* about Martin." Fern shook her head slowly. "No one dares intrude on your privacy. But…"

"My privacy? What does that have to do with Martin? What has happened?" Cassie's panic rose.

For years she'd worried terrible news would come about

Martin. Ever since he left with his brother three years ago, she'd prayed for him each and every day.

Martin was such a gentle soul. To her, it felt as if he'd gone out among the wolves by leaving the safety of their community and the family and friends who loved him. So, when he'd finally come back last summer to help build Nick and Fern's new house above their store, Cassie had allowed herself the smallest of hopes that he might still come back to Promise to stay.

Only his visits had been short and far between ever since. And now, something had happened to Martin that had his sister's face scrunched up with concern.

"*Nay*, Martin is fine," the woman stated matter-of-factly, much to Cassie's relief. "What I mean is that I think Martin is the reason Eli doesn't want you to use the farmhouse for your bakery."

"That doesn't make any sense. What does Martin have to do with me using Uncle Nick's farmhouse for my bakery?"

Fern's mouth dropped open briefly. "You really don't know, do you? I thought… I guess we all assumed that he would have told you."

So, they were all in on some sort of secret, after all.

"You have to tell me, Fern. What is it that no one is sharing with me—including Martin?"

"Relax, Martin." Uncle Titus flipped the turn signal of his farm truck to show they were exiting the highway onto the mountain road leading to Promise, Virginia. "Your bees are fine back there. It's still dark, so the bees are sleeping. I've gone slow, the air is cool and we'll be at the farm in twenty minutes."

"*Ya. Ya.* I know." His uncle had systematically gone through the checklist of Martin's concerns for his precious cargo. Sure, he'd transported beehives many times, but never as far as today. He gripped his fingers around his knees to keep them still. He didn't realize he'd been stimming.

That's what the Mennonite counselor called the hand flapping movements and other tics that soothed him when he was anxious. The problem was they had the opposite effect on people around him. And he'd learned to control them. Mostly.

Martin inhaled deeply to settle his nerves. "I really appreciate your help with this."

"I'm happy to do it. A quick visit with family is overdue on my part." His father's brother had grown up Old Order Amish in the Virginia Highlands, just like Martin had. But he'd moved down to the valley and joined a group of Beachy Amish, who dressed and worshipped Plain but used electricity and drove black, simple vehicles.

Martin had considered joining their church down in the valley until last summer when he'd helped his sister out of a pinch by leasing their farmhouse, even though he had no intention of living in it. After an exceptional honey harvest two years running, it had been something useful he was in a unique position to do. So he had.

He only meant to keep the property in the family until his nieces and nephews grew up. Ever since, though, he'd felt a tug back to his old home.

And it was an odd sensation he didn't understand or like, in particular. He'd left Promise with his twin brother, Seth, because they'd never felt they belonged there. Trouble was, Seth had moved on down to Florida while Martin stayed with his bees in the Shenandoah Valley.

Being by himself wasn't so bad, really. In fact, alone worked best for him.

This trip was simply to set up his beehives and give collecting mountain honey a try. And before his *mamm* or Cassie Weaver got any ideas that he might stay, he'd be on his way back down the mountain.

"Looks like there's a light on." Uncle Titus stared ahead at the farmhouse. Martin strained his eyes against the dim predawn in the same direction. Sure enough, a faint glow emanated from the kitchen window.

"Strange. No one mentioned anyone staying here." He knew non-Amish often left on electric lights when a home was empty, but none of his family would be foolish enough to leave gas lights on unattended. "Well, whoever it is, I need to alert them to what we're doing. I don't want someone wandering up on us while we unload the bees. Especially not as we reopen the hives and let them out."

"*Nay*. We don't want anyone getting stung." His uncle eased the truck to the end of the driveway near the house, rather than through the pasture gate as they'd planned, and shut off the engine.

Martin had planned every meticulous detail of this move. Surprises like this twisted his already frayed nerves into an expanding knot of buzzing loose ends. "I'll be right back."

"Don't get too grumpy with whatever poor soul is in that kitchen. It's not their fault this job requires so much fussy attention on your end." Titus chuckled, then removed his seat belt. "Maybe I'll just come along for *goot* measure."

"I'm not that bad." Although Martin had to admit to himself, he sounded pretty gruff already.

He sighed and reminded himself that everything would work out fine. Probably. Hopefully. Maybe. He kicked at the gravel. Who really knew?

As he crossed the last step up to the porch, the scent of cinnamon, yeast and honey wafted in the air. He hadn't smelled that combination in years. Somewhere around three years, to be exact.

"Whoo-boy! Don't that make your mouth water?" Uncle Titus grinned as wide as one of the giant cinnamon rolls Martin had just been reminded of—the ones Cassie used to bake and glaze with a honey concoction just for him.

Martin rapped lightly on the front door, then momentarily the kitchen curtain pulled back, revealing the sweet face of Cassie Weaver, the minister's daughter and his childhood friend.

"Well, well, what do you know? Seems I could have stayed in that nice, warm truck after all." His uncle elbowed him right under the rib cage, an altogether unpleasant sensation that made him jump. "Appears to me, some young woman has her *kapp* set on you. Every Amish woman knows the way to a man's heart is through his stomach."

"It's Cassie." Martin inhaled a deep breath for patience. Cassie was a friend—once his best friend—everyone knew that. If she'd been more, which she definitely wasn't, he may have stayed in the first place. "I can promise you that her intention is not anything like that."

Although Cassie showing up with cinnamon buns was admittedly suspicious.

"I reckon we're about to find out, aren't we?" His uncle wagged his eyebrows and Martin looked away. Why did people persist in making comments like that about him and Cassie? They were friends, plain and simple.

While he was confident Cassie had no romantic intentions, Martin couldn't fathom what her real reason was for being at the farmhouse baking his favorite treat before the sun came up. But he knew it all added up to one thing— namely, she wanted a favor.

And as always, she knew just how to get him to agree

with her—before he even knew what she wanted. Those cinnamon buns did the trick. Every. Time.

Cassie let the curtain drop back in place and straightened her shoulders. So far, so good. *Gott* bless Fern for alerting her of Martin's plans to bring some of his beehives to Promise for making mountain honey.

She wasn't sure what made mountain honey different from any other honey, although over the years she'd listened to Martin enough to know the flowers the bees visited affected the flavor of the honey they produced. Whatever it meant, she was just glad it brought Martin back up the mountain to Promise.

A dreadful shiver ran up her spine. Except for the bees. She wasn't too pleased about more bees. But she supposed the hives would be far away from the house. Out of sight and out of mind, where she preferred they remain.

Carrying a plateful of the cinnamon bun recipe dubbed the Martin Special, she made her way to the front door to greet him and his uncle. How *wunnerbar* that in less than twenty-four hours since her *datt* asked her to wait before opening her bakery in this very house, her plans were so quickly about to take a turn for the better.

Ya, Martin's arrival today was nothing less than providential. If anyone would see things her way about the bakery, Martin would.

With a welcoming smile, she opened the door.

"*Goot Mariye*, Titus." Martin's uncle stood closest to the door. His eyes were round, and he appeared ready to dive headlong into the mound of cinnamon rolls she held before him. She glanced over Titus's shoulder, making eye contact with Martin. "Hello, Martin. I've made your favorite."

"*Ya*, I see." He started to smile then looked away as if she held a plateful of temptation. "I only stopped by the house so as not to frighten whoever was here. We're just heading to one of the back pastures to set up some hives." He tugged at his uncle's sleeve. "*Kumm*, there's no time. You'll have to get one of those rolls after we set up the hives."

Titus snatched a bun off the plate. "He's in a dither about them bees. You'll have to excuse his rudeness."

Already about to descend the first step off the porch, Martin paused. His shoulders sagged, and he turned back to face her like a wayward child forced to apologize by his *mamm*.

This was not promising. Not at all. And far from the reaction she had hoped for.

"I'm sorry, Cassie. But we really can't waste a minute." He looked down at his feet and shoved his hands in his pockets.

Cassie hated that he felt so uncomfortable. He wasn't supposed to feel that way with her. Other people made him nervous, but she was his friend. Wasn't she? More might have changed between them than she thought.

"Of course. I understand."

Slowly his eyes, green as the new spring grass, came back to meet hers. "I'll come back."

His words sounded more like a tortuous concession than the pleasure he normally showed for her treats. And she'd been up two hours early this morning to make them for him. *Vell*, maybe not *just* for him. She did have a reason.

Titus had made his way back toward the truck, but Martin was waiting for her reply. She tried to smile over her disappointment. "Just don't take as long to come back as the last time you made that promise. My cinnamon buns won't last three years."

Understanding dawned in his expression. His somber

look changed to a smile. "Don't worry, Cass. Your special recipe is as irresistible as ever."

Cass—his friendly shortened version of her name—sparked some hope in her heart.

Martin was still her friend, and he'd help her. She only had to get him to stay in Promise long enough to do so. The plate of cinnamon buns weighed heavily in her hands. They may have lost some of their usual instant charm on him, but she wasn't giving up yet.

Chapter Two

Cassie watched the sunrise expand its colors across the mountain ridge into a brightening sky. Shadowed waves stretched across the hillsides, whose trees had only just begun to bud and awaken from their winter dormancy.

Waiting for Martin Beiler was becoming a terrible habit, Cass decided as she waited on the porch for him to return from setting up his hives.

The hot buns she'd made for him were barely warm now. Soon they'd be cold. Full daylight had almost broken, and she was late for work. Her baking routine at the store was going to be off schedule. If she didn't hurry, there'd be no fresh bread ready for the lunch rush at the deli counter.

She should have told Martin to come to the store for his cinnamon rolls when he was done, but he probably wouldn't have obliged.

He'd appeared eager to take care of his bees and be gone. Again. And apparently, he'd snuck into Promise before to prepare the hive sites and then slipped right back out without so much as a hello or a goodbye to her. If Fern hadn't noticed he was there on one of her walks, no one might've known at all.

It was a Martin kind of thing to keep his comings and goings private. But she'd been the first person he'd sought out in the past. No wonder everyone assumed she knew more than she did about what he was up to. Word had spread quickly through their families about his plans for the bees here on the farm. Normally, she would have known before they did. But not this time.

Why?

Maybe he didn't want to get her hopes up that he might move back to stay. Truthfully, she already had—as much as she dared, which was very little.

Three years ago, she'd cried when he and Seth left home, and made Martin promise to come back. The memory of her silly eighteen-year-old self that day made her cringe. She'd taken his choice to leave so personally—not only did he feel like he didn't belong in their community, but that their friendship wasn't worth staying for, either. At least, that's how she'd taken it.

She'd grown up enough to know that everything wasn't about her, and that Martin really had needed to discover where he belonged. Still, she wasn't convinced he'd found what he was looking for down in the valley. If anything, it sounded to her like he spent more time alone than ever. She couldn't help but still believe he belonged in Promise, just like she'd argued before he left.

And it stung that he no longer considered her part of his private circle enough to tell her what was going on. For him, that circle had always been small. Sometimes so small, it only included the two of them.

Not anymore, it seemed.

Hence the cinnamon buns. They'd always put Martin in an exceptionally good mood before. His odd reaction this morning was either worry over those bees, as Titus had said, or something else was afoot.

She just wanted her friend back.

Ach, vell...she wanted her own bakery, too. And she had an idea that might get both things at once.

Martin was the perfect solution to the pesky disagreement with her *datt* about the safety of opening her bakery at the farm. She wanted her *datt*'s blessing and maybe—just maybe—her *datt* would agree, if Martin went along with her idea.

He already had a place to live, and now he even had some of his bees here.

What was there to hold him back from staying a while? His fear of people, most likely.

Alright, so maybe Martin wasn't the perfect candidate, considering she hoped for a lot of traffic through her shop. But by her guess, Martin would do whatever it took to help a friend. If he still considered her one.

Another minor hiccup in this plan.

But if by helping her, Martin stayed around for more than a passing visit, he might figure out he belonged here all along with family and friends and a community. No one should be alone. Especially not someone as kind as Martin.

The whole plan was a win-win for them both. Although she'd have to be patient—probably the toughest part of the entire plan. But, she'd already waited on Martin for three years, so...

Wait?

What had Fern said? Her *datt*'s worries had everything to do with Martin. It still didn't make sense. *You really don't know? Everyone assumed...*

Did their families believe there was more between her and Martin than their eternal friendship?

Nay. How ridiculous.

But if they did?

Delight tickled her at the brilliance of her newly forming plan—minus a few complications she'd worry about later.

She couldn't wait to get started. And these cinnamon buns that got her out of bed an extra hour early weren't going to waste.

Balancing two plates—one for Martin and the other for Titus—laden with honey-coated cinnamon buns in one hand and a thermos of hot cocoa in the other, Cassie followed the flattened grass trail left by the truck tires to find the men. The air was no longer cool enough to create white puffs of cloud from her breath, and the uphill climb was warming her blood fast.

Martin and his bees couldn't be much farther. She frowned at the thought of the tiny insects with their tiny but painful stingers. The only piece of information she'd found valuable over the years was that smoke made them sleepy, or go back to their hive, or something. Whatever it was, it was a good thing. Somehow, it kept them from stinging.

And Martin always had that smoker with him when he handled bees. Plus, she'd stay back at a safe distance.

So, she'd be fine. Right?

A white veiled hat bobbed in and out of view across the next hilltop. That had to be Martin at work. She approached from the wood line, hoping to remain as far out of the way as possible.

Martin waved at her. Or maybe he was signaling her to move, but which way? She couldn't tell, and then he made a clear sign for her to stop.

She froze. Had she gotten too close to the bees? Martin knew how much they frightened her. She glanced around but all the hives were at least fifty feet away. Hopefully, he would head in her direction soon.

She was standing in a patch of white phlox, the first she'd

noticed in bloom, a *goot* sign that spring was underway. Looking up, she noticed Martin headed her way—finally. His pace was calm and manner sedate, so surely everything was alright.

She relaxed a little at the sight of the blessed smoke machine in his hand.

That tin can with the pointy cap and small bellows attached to the side made her feel safe. Martin was cautious like that. And she appreciated it. He had to know how little she wanted to be out here anywhere near so many bees, even if they made such *wunnerbar goot* honey.

"Cass." Martin called to her from about ten feet away. "Do. Not. Run. Don't even move."

Only then did she hear the buzz swirling above her.

One, two, three…four honeybees dropped straight down onto the plates she held in front of her like a weapon. A very useless one.

Oh, dear, her *datt* might be right. Maybe this was not a *goot* location for her bakery. Too frightened to move, she pinned her focus on Martin.

"Cass, put the plates down. Very, very slowly. Don't make any sudden movements. Then, as easy as you can, leave it on the ground."

"How?" Her voice shook, and her hands tremored, as the golden-brown buns quickly turned into a pile of black and yellow.

"You can do it. Bend your knees. Easy. That's it. Now, keep the bees focused on the honey."

How was she supposed to do that? "I can't."

"You are doing it. They want the honey, so just give it to them without threatening them."

Threaten *them*! She was the one terrified for her life, as she crouched down as far as her legs would allow and rested the plates on the ground. The buzzing above her head was so loud now she could feel the vibrations in her heart.

"Don't move away too fast. The slower you go, the better."

That didn't seem right. In fact, the opposite had to be true. Everything in her wanted to race back over that hill as fast as she could.

And never come back.

Forget the bakery. Forget Martin.

Just run.

A bee swarm in springtime wasn't unusual. This one was happily huddled on that tree branch when he'd arrived earlier. And until Cassie walked up, his only concern had been how he could draw them into a hive to keep them.

Her fear of bees was why he'd asked her to wait at the house. When things took longer than expected, he wasn't the least surprised to see her coming over the hill. But only Cassie could land her bee-fearing self right under a wild swarm and with an armload of the bees' most prized possession, to boot.

She wasn't allergic, thankfully. Still, his primary focus was to prevent her from getting stung. But the harried look in her eyes showed she was about to run.

"Don't even think about it, Cass. They're faster than you. You can't outrun them. Please trust me. All they want right now is that honey. But if you make any sudden moves, they might attack."

Her dark brown eyes widened, and her pupils dilated. Attack may have been a bad word choice.

"You're so close to being safe. Just do what you did before, but in reverse. Pull your arms back toward your body, then I'll smoke them so you can come here to me. Just don't run. Okay?"

Clearly too petrified to answer out loud, she still managed to follow his directions in super slow motion.

"I knew you could do it." He gave a gentle puff of smoke toward the bees. Mostly to make Cassie feel better. Her sweet confections already had the bees well distracted. He was a tad jealous. He'd been looking forward to eating those himself.

Cassie came behind him and gripped the edges of his suit, clinging to him as if she was in mortal danger. He led her away and knew she was feeling safer as her hold on him loosened.

He glanced around for his uncle and spotted him in the pickup with his head lolled to one side, taking a nap. Martin was tired, too, but there was still more work to be done. He needed to go to his parents' farm and see if he had supplies there to build a hive to attract and house that swarm.

But first things first.

He turned to face Cassie. "Did you get stung?"

"Nay." She shook her head. Her wavy black hair that always had a wild nature of its own was springing out in coils from under her prayer *kapp*. She stepped back from him. "How can you grin like that at me? This is not funny, Martin Beiler."

"I wasn't. It isn't… I know." He hadn't meant to grin. But her hair. Cassie had changed since he left, not in a bad way. She'd matured. He certainly had, especially after learning about his autism and how to cope with it. But that one thing—her untamable hair—had remained the same. He was glad.

And now he was completely distracted.

"I have to get to work. I'm late." Annoyance laced her voice. She sure had recovered from her shock in a hurry.

"We were packing up to leave, when you…" He shrugged,

deciding it was wiser not to finish that statement. "You could ride with us. I have to go over to *Mamm* and *Datt*'s, but we can drop you off first." Plus, he wanted time to explain that it wasn't his bees that had bothered her. He didn't know what difference that made exactly, except he couldn't stand her being put out with him like this. Of course, if she hadn't shown up with two plates full of honey and sugar...

"*Ya*, that would save time." She looked warily toward the truck. "Is it safe over there?"

He waved the smoker like a magician's wand. "Not that we'll need this. But I promise I can get you safely to the truck."

A short minute later, Cassie stood safely beside the tailgate as he removed his protective gear and put away the last of his supplies. With one hip propped up against the truck, she watched him finish until he turned to face her.

In contrast to her frizzing hair, her apron remained starchy smooth. Then, he noticed a fingerprint of white flour against the plum-colored shoulder of her dress, as if she'd swiped at something and left a trail behind. Two years younger and six inches shorter than Martin, she had her *datt*'s dark looks but not his height. And she was looking up at Martin with a big question behind her brown eyes.

"You love your beekeeping, don't you?" she asked in a casual tone.

"*Ya*." He hesitated. Was this going to be about defending what he did? Because he didn't have time for that. He needed to get back here with supplies before that swarm invaded one of his established hives.

"I understand." Her fingers reached out to rest gently against his forearm, as light as a feather across his skin, before she pulled away. "That's how I feel about baking. Well, about having my own bakery."

Martin relaxed against the tailgate. He could afford to talk about something this important to her for a minute. "You should do it, Cass. You do make the best cinnamon buns I've ever tasted."

She smiled, and he was glad she no longer seemed angry at him. "Your bees think so, too."

"Those aren't my bees. Not yet, anyway." He watched her head tilt in question. "I'll explain later. So, are you going to open your own bakery? Lots of Amish women run their own businesses now."

"That's what I wanted to talk to you about." She tapped a finger against her chin.

"Ah, I see. Here comes the cinnamon bun favor." His mouth turned up into a grin again, but she didn't recoil this time. "Only trouble is, I haven't gotten to eat one yet."

"There are plenty more. But you seem in a hurry. And I'm late for work." She placed a hand on her hip and smiled widely up at him. "How about you come to supper tonight, and we can discuss everything over dessert?"

He hadn't planned to stay that long. "I think Uncle Titus has to get back home."

It was a lame excuse but not invalid.

"Don't blame me." His uncle's voice called out from the front of the truck. "I have some visiting to do. And your *grossmammi* was already on my case to stay the night."

Martin shifted his weight from one foot to the other. Of course, *Gammi* wanted her son to stay longer. But that wasn't the agreement. Still, he might need a little time to make sure all went well with this new hive.

"Well?" Cassie raised an eyebrow at him.

One night. One supper. What harm could it do? That didn't mean he was moving back to stay. "What time do you get off work? I'll come walk you home for supper."

"Five o'clock, usually, but I'll be late today. Can you come at six? Supper is always at half past six."

"Six, it is," he agreed.

Her feet skipped a little dance ahead of him to the front of the truck. As he climbed into the bench seat beside her, he whispered, "But there had better be honey-smothered, hot cinnamon buns on the table."

"As long as you don't bring any bees." She made a face with an exaggerated shiver, as he slipped into the truck beside her.

Martin clicked his seat belt into the latch as his uncle turned the truck around, muttering something under his breath about the folly of youth and the games they played.

Cassie looked at him as if wondering what his uncle was talking about.

Martin shrugged.

People said strange things, even more so whenever Cassie was involved in the topic. Actually, he didn't think he wanted to know what his uncle meant. Undoubtedly, it would be embarrassing, and he was thankful Cassie didn't seem to understand, either.

She was sitting there looking very pleased with herself, clearly recovered fully from her scare.

Martin's skin tingled, making him scratch a spot above his elbow. What had he gotten himself into? With Cassie there was no telling.

Chapter Three

Waiting for Martin outside Weaver's Amish Store, Cassie paced from one side of the driveway entrance to the other. Nick and Fern had already left, and she hoped Martin showed up before another member of one of their families drove by in a buggy and offered her a ride. She had to warn him—privately—that supper had turned into a major event.

She'd invited Martin to an ordinary weeknight supper at her parents' house. Not a giant family conference disguised as a meal.

And yet, that's what appeared to be happening. And not only with the extended Weaver family, but an extra pile of Beilers had been thrown into the mix, as well.

Didn't they know this was exactly the kind of overcrowded spectacle that would send Martin hightailing it straight back down the mountain?

Sure, she believed Martin needed friends and family and community in order to find belonging. And all of those things were what made Promise such a special place. Only sometimes they took it too far.

Now, for instance.

She sure wouldn't mind skipping this supper. Maybe she and Martin could disappear together to whatever quiet corner of the world Martin liked to hide in. Cassie needed people more than her friend seemed to, but she had missed those quieter moments with him.

Not that Martin was silent. He made her laugh more than anyone else. And he knew so many interesting things. Being with Martin was never dull.

Peaceful was how she'd describe being with him. He craved peace, which also explained what he'd done for his family last year. But then he suffered, too. Things she never noticed much caused him severe irritation at times.

Loud noises and lots of people were at the top of that list.

Ach, what a mess she was in now.

A pickup truck she recognized from that morning came to a stop at the corner. Martin's grandmother, Ada, was in the front seat with his uncle, but there was no sign of Martin.

"He'll be down shortly," Titus hollered out the window, sounding as much a Virginian as an Amish man. "See y'all at supper."

Cassie couldn't help but smile back at Titus's enthusiasm, even if he did appear to look forward to supper like a child on his way to the circus more than a grown man going to a family meal. He and Ada waved happily as they drove down the street.

Ya, Ada was in matchmaker heaven. She'd gotten Fern and Nick together. Now, Martin was likely next on her list of *kins-kinnah* to marry off. Just wait until Titus's *kinner* were old enough for her to interfere. He might not be smiling so brightly at that circus.

Resigned to the fact a family show was exactly what awaited her, Cassie headed up the lane toward the farm to meet up with Martin on his way. She didn't have to go far before he came into view. Hands in his pockets, he studied the ground as he walked. The setting sun caught the dark blond curls sneaking out from under his hat.

Her heart gave a little flip at the familiar sight. Only because she'd missed him being around. She didn't have any silly school-girl feelings. Not anymore. Not since she turned sixteen and he never once invited her to a singing.

Of course, he didn't attend those social functions, either. Not if he could help it. Still, those awkward feelings were in the past and had nothing to do with the butterflies in her stomach now.

Nay, that was definitely nervousness about the fiasco of a supper coming up.

"*Denki* for coming," she offered as he came to a stop in front of her. "I wouldn't blame you if you'd changed your mind."

He looked her full in the face, then. His body cast a shadow across her, making it hard to read his expression. "I promised, didn't I?"

Ya. And Martin kept his promises.

"Still… I'm sorry for how it's turned out. I saw your *gammi* and *onkel* headed that way, so I reckon you know it's turned into a big brouhaha."

"Brouhaha." He echoed the word. Even in the shadows, she couldn't mistake the grin that spread across his face or the laugh that rumbled up from deep in his belly. "Now, that's a *goot* word for it, if it means what it sounds like. Where'd you learn that one?"

She shrugged, unwilling to mention the *Englisch* romance novels she liked to borrow from the library. "If the shoe fits…or in this case, the word."

"I expect brouhaha will be a perfect fit." He offered her his arm, exactly like one of the lords in those novels might do, revealing that he hadn't forgotten her secret pastime. "We should get going."

Hoping the low light hid the blush flaming her cheeks, she placed her hand on his arm and walked beside him.

"Don't worry too much about me, Cass. This kind of thing isn't my favorite way to spend an evening, but I can handle it."

"Maybe you've forgotten what it's like." She looked over at him. "I'm not sure *I* can deal with it."

He laughed again. "You can handle anything. And I didn't mean I could take it all the time. But I can do it this once for you."

Ach, those pesky butterflies had to stop. She knew he didn't mean it the way it sounded. Walking in the sunset and holding his arm just had her mixed up. She let go to help keep her senses.

"*Denki*, Martin. And before we have an audience, maybe I should explain the reason I made the Martin Special this morning."

"*Ya*, I think you should. I'd rather be prepared. So what's the cinnamon-bun favor this time?" There was a smile in his voice that eased the tension she'd been feeling all afternoon.

"It's simple, really. I want to run a bakery from Uncle Nick's… I mean, your farmhouse kitchen."

"It's not mine. I guess someone told you about the lease. It's complicated. But also simple. The farm will go to Fern and Nick. I'm just filling in the gap so they can have it for their *kinner* when the time comes. But I don't want anyone calling it mine. I'd much rather folks still think of it as their family's place."

She was getting sidetracked from her plan for the bakery, but she had to say something. "I just wish you had felt like you could tell me, so I didn't have to hear it from someone else."

He paused his steps for a moment. "I trust you, Cassie. I honestly didn't think to tell you about the farm because it was just something I felt I had to do. And that was the end of it. At least until I decided to put some hive yards up there." He didn't want credit for what he'd done. He'd always been a humble person.

His finger brushed her elbow ever so slightly. "I didn't mean to offend you."

"*Denki*. That makes me feel better. I was afraid we weren't friends anymore."

"*Ach*, Cassie. You're still my best friend." He smiled down at her and then resumed their walk.

Her heart sank. His best friend. How could that be? He hadn't spent more than a few hours with her in over three years. This was worse than she imagined. His inner circle had shrunk to one—himself.

"Martin Beiler!" Cassie whirled around to face him so fast that he almost walked straight into her, but that wasn't going to slow her down. "Do you truly stay so off to yourself? If I'm your best friend, then you better show your face around here a lot more."

He sighed. "And I suspect this favor of yours is a plan to remedy that."

"How did you know? Never mind, don't answer. We are almost home, and I need to fill you in." She made a quick decision to leave out her suspicion that their families believed they were secretly courting. Somehow saying that out loud—and to Martin—was far too embarrassing. Besides, she wanted him to stay, not run. The idea of a secret courtship was sure to cause the latter.

And now, success was more important than she had thought, not only for her bakery, but to save Martin from becoming a total recluse.

* * *

Twelve adults and an assortment of young siblings and cousins gathered around Eli Weaver's table with their heads bowed in silent prayer. Even for a minister, Cassie's father appeared more solemn than usual this evening.

Martin's mouth tasted like sawdust, and he wished he'd taken a sip of water when he had the chance before their thanksgiving for the food had begun.

The way Cassie had explained things to him sounded simple. She wanted to open her bakery in the farmhouse. Everyone was on board except Eli, who felt it was too remote and unsafe for her to work there all alone. Martin found that a reasonable concern, too, but not an insurmountable one.

Cassie's idea was for Martin to move in at the farm until she could afford to hire employees. So easy.

For her.

There hadn't been time to bring up the flaws in this plan, and Martin was sure Eli would do that part for him. There hadn't been time to explain a lot of things. He'd had a very enlightening discussion with his uncle that afternoon.

What he knew for certain was that he would do his best to help Cassie get her bakery started. A solution couldn't be that difficult to come up with. Although, he'd much prefer to figure it out between himself, Cassie and Eli over a cinnamon bun than around this sixteen-foot-long dining table.

Eli cleared his throat, heads raised and the passing of the food began.

A cinnamon bun had better be waiting for him later because there was no way his stomach could handle food until all this was over. He took some meager portions and kept the serving bowls moving away from him, all the while wondering who would broach the subject on everyone's minds first.

Cassie sat next to Martin, then her grandparents and her *mamm* ranged down the side to the head of the table where Eli sat. Across from Martin were Nick and Fern, then Martin's *mamm* and *datt* near the head of the table. At the far end of the table were his uncle, grandmother and the assorted rest of the *kinner* who belonged to all the adults.

"Well, Martin, what brings you to Promise this time?" Eli asked from the head of the table, about four seats away.

"Bees."

"Hmm." Eli rubbed his beard and looked from Martin to Cassie.

"He's moving into the farmhouse," she announced.

Glad his mouth was empty, or else he'd have choked, Martin reached for his water glass.

"So, there's no need to worry about the farm being a safe place anymore. Martin will protect me."

"From the bees?"

"What? *Nay, Datt*. From whoever—whatever—you were worried about. It's all taken care of now."

"What about the bees?"

Martin couldn't tell if Eli was asking him or Cassie about the bees, but maybe it was time for him to step in, regardless. "The bees aren't a danger to Cassie. They're far away from the house, and there are methods of ensuring that even if she were to get stung, it wouldn't hurt her." She wouldn't like those methods and would probably never agree to them, but it was true.

He suddenly realized the room was perfectly silent again, maybe quieter than during prayer.

Cassie's mouth was hanging open, and Eli was rubbing

his temples with his forefingers. Martin wasn't positive, but he thought maybe in an effort not to laugh.

After another beat of silence and a deep breath, Eli went on. "Is this a temporary or a permanent move?"

"Permanent," Cassie interjected.

"Temporary," Martin corrected.

Cassie bumped her leg against his under the table. He bumped hers back.

"Well, which one?"

Cassie shot him a pleading look, but he wasn't going to lie. "Just long enough to help Cassie get her business running well enough to hire help, so she won't be alone."

"No one should be alone," Cassie muttered for only him to hear.

"I might be able to go along with this," Eli started, then paused to make clear eye contact with Martin. "A permanent move would bring some…well, some challenges." His gaze darted briefly to his daughter, then back to Martin.

By challenges, Eli meant joining the church for one. Sharing a house with an unmarried woman, even if only during the daytime. *Ya*, all the things Cassie so easily overlooked.

Maintaining eye contact this long took a great deal of effort, but he'd promised Cassie he'd do his best to help her. And people didn't trust you if you couldn't look them in the eye. No matter how hard that was for someone with autism.

"I have over two hundred hives to care for all over the valley. And even though I'd like to have more here in the mountains, I have to manage my hives in the valley, as well. I'll stay to help Cassie, but that is the best I can do."

Cassie slumped in her chair.

But Eli's stance relaxed. He might have even smiled for a second.

Strange that.

The more Martin held his ground about only staying in Promise temporarily, the less Eli opposed Cassie's idea.

Work with the bees. A successful beekeeper watches and learns from the bees more than the books.

"How long will you stay?" Eli asked.

Cassie thought her new bakery hinged on Martin agreeing to her plan. It didn't. Eli was the key. Cassie wouldn't do anything as major as this without her *datt*'s blessing, which Martin respected. And her *datt* wouldn't agree to anything he didn't believe in his daughter's best interest. He respected that, too.

"Martin?" Cassie nudged him for an answer to Eli's question.

He cleared his throat. "I can only manage to stay three months, max."

He ignored the instant jab to his leg and the huff Cassie made beside him and remained focused on Eli's reaction.

"Alright, then, Cassie. You have my blessing." Eli smiled at his daughter, and slowly the hum around the table revived and moved to other topics.

Pleased with his successful negotiation on her behalf, Martin turned to Cassie, expecting a smile. Instead, her eyes looked watery and her mouth turned down.

What had he done wrong now?

"Three months? Martin, that's not enough time. Not at all." Her voice was a whisper as she excused herself from the table.

His momentary victory dropped like a stone to the bottom of his gut.

How was he supposed to explain to her what his uncle had shared with him that afternoon? He hadn't had the nerve to tell her on their walk over that he knew why the entire clan had come to supper tonight.

Everyone around this table—with the important exception of Cassie and himself—believed the two of them had some kind of secret courtship going on. The potential of his moving back had both families expecting an engagement announcement at any time. He couldn't let them continue to believe that. For Cassie's sake more than his own.

And now that they knew better, they'd be matchmaking by morning.

Except for Eli. Her *datt* was wholly relieved when Martin said the move was temporary.

And that was the leverage Martin had to use to keep his promise to her.

Cassie was upset with him, but Martin's counselor sure was going to be impressed that he'd figured out this tangled web of human emotion.

He couldn't explain how he understood Eli Weaver at that moment, except that they agreed on at least one thing. Martin wasn't right for Cassie.

Nay, more than one.

Like Eli, Martin would also do whatever it took to protect Cassie and make her happy.

Chapter Four

"A secret courtship. Are you sure?" Cassie stared at Martin, trying to decide if he was teasing her. He'd slipped in the back entrance to Uncle Nick's store to tell her some far-fetched tale about how all their relatives believed they were going to make an announcement last night about their engagement.

She'd immediately had to rein in her runaway imagination that wandered off to a place where an engagement to Martin might be real. *Ach*, she knew better. And so must everyone else. No matter how hard she'd tried to hide it, maybe folks had known she was a little sweet on Martin growing up. Still, jumping to the conclusion that Martin had been secretly courting her on his rare visits to Promise was a generous leap of assumptions. But getting engaged already?

"I reckon they got tired of all the same old tall tales they like to tell around here and made up a new one." He shrugged. Mountain folk plus Amish folk surely did make for some wild storytelling. Still, she couldn't believe this one.

"That's not a very *goot* joke. Martin." She dumped a ball of pastry dough onto the well-floured countertop and immediately regretted the action. A poof of white dust smacked her in the face.

Martin, who was to blame for the distraction leading to the mess she'd made, was biting the inside of his cheek to keep from laughing at her.

"It's not funny." She swiped at the powder clinging to her eyebrows, only to realize she'd now wiped sticky dough across her forehead, too.

Martin held his stomach as if he might bust. She tried to glare, but a laugh bubbled out of her instead.

In a wink, they were both laughing as she tried to clean her face with a damp tea towel. After a decent attempt to make herself presentable, she wiped her face one last time and held her head up for Martin to see.

"Better?"

He swallowed and took a step back from her before answering, "*Ya.* You look…fine." But he was still looking at her in a way that made her pulse skitter.

Cassie pushed aside the feeling. The ridiculous notion of being engaged to Martin had ruined her sense of reality. This had to stop. No good would come of dwelling on something that didn't exist.

"I suppose you had a reason to stop by so early. One other than to tease me." She did her best to sound unaffected by the moment.

"I came to see… I came to see if you'd like to come with us down the mountain." Martin wasn't looking at her anymore. "Probably not a *goot* idea, considering… But *Mamm* is coming and asked if you'd keep her company."

"You're going back?" Cassie tried to rein back on the panic she heard in her voice. But she didn't understand. "You promised just last night you'd stay."

Calm as usual, Martin remained matter-of-fact. "Titus has to get home. And I need to bring my things, if I'm going to stay for a while." His eyes met hers with a flicker of worry. "I'll have to check on a few of my hives before leaving them, but you wouldn't have to come along for that."

He seemed to ask out of duty to his *mamm*, like he was holding his breath in hopes she'd decline.

"I can't just leave," she told him and waved her hand toward all the baking she had to do for the day. "But I'd like to. I've often wondered what your life is like down in the valley."

He smiled at that. "I'd be happy to show you. But today is probably not the best time. Not because you can't come. I have a hunch my *mamm* and *schwester* are handling that issue right now." His brows drew together. "You don't seem to believe me, but I'm not teasing you, Cass."

"*Vell*, it is hard to believe that we'd be the last to know about our own...about such a thing." She couldn't get the word *engagement* to come out.

"True."

Two terribly long heartbeats passed between them. She wanted to laugh to break the tension, but she wasn't going to mock the idea of a romantic relationship with Martin. He didn't seem inclined to make light of it, either. All of which left her both relieved and thankful, with no idea what to say next.

Just then, Fern walked through the staff door and tied an apron around her protruding middle. "You two better get along. They're outside waiting for you." Fern smiled widely, and Cassie knew a conspiracy was underfoot.

She glanced at Martin, who gave her a helpless shrug. His family, or at least his *mamm* and his sister, were colluding against them. Or maybe *for* them.

"You weren't joking, were you?" she whispered.

He shook his head.

A secret courtship. Of all the ridiculous notions. Martin

was no more wooing her than…she didn't know what. But of course Fern would want Martin to come back to Promise as much as Cassie did. And if she believed marriage was the best way to get him to stay, she'd do what she could to encourage him along.

Ideas began to spark faster than flint on dry leaves. This could work in her favor, after all. With Fern and his *mamm*, Leah Beiler, working on her side, Cassie stood a much better chance at keeping Martin in Promise longer than three months. Permanently, even.

"Cass?" Martin interrupted the flickering flames of a new plan coming to life in her mind.

"Vass?" She looked up at him.

"Are you coming or not?" He was eyeing the back door and scratching his elbow. The situation was making him nervous.

She knew marriage to her was far from Martin's mind, but she needed all the time with him she could get to show him how much better off he'd be back in Promise.

"Ya, of course. I'd love to come." For good measure, she batted her eyelashes at Fern, who startled slightly at the gesture.

Oops. She'd have to work on her flirting skills—and aim them in the right direction. Only it wasn't Martin she needed to convince. She just needed everyone else to continue thinking she and Martin were lovebirds about to marry.

Truly, she was unsure what exactly she was doing, but had the entire ride down the mountain and back to work out her strategy.

"What was that?" Martin asked under his breath after the back door closed behind them. "The last thing we should do is encourage this misunderstanding. I'll have you know, it's not just my family who are scheming. Yours are in it, too." He scuffed the bottom of his shoe against the gravel and turned to face her just out of earshot of his uncle and *mamm* waiting at the truck in the parking lot. "The whole church is gossiping about us, Cass. This is not a joke. I promise you."

The mention of gossip soured her spirits. She hated gossip. "You know I don't listen to gossip. All it does is cause trouble and hurt people."

All of which made her budding idea even better. Why not use the others' meddling to her advantage for a change? She clamped a hand around Martin's wrist to stop him getting any closer to the truck.

"Trust me, Martin. I have a plan. Everything is going to work out just how it is meant to be. You'll see."

"Cass, I don't think you understand."

"Don't worry. I know you don't feel that way about me, Martin. And that's okay." She did her best to sound much more mature than the girl who had cried over him three years ago and hoped he didn't detect how much the sting of it remained even now.

Instead of relieved or reassured, as Cassie hoped he would be, Martin massaged his forehead with his thumb and forefinger. "Cass…"

"Dear me!" Leah Beiler came bustling toward them. "I'm afraid the cabin of that truck is *zu glay* for all of us to fit." She pinched her fingers together to imitate a small space. "For sure and certain, there's no room for me. You two hop on in." She motioned them both forward. "I know Titus is eager to get on the road. I'll go help Fern with the *kinner* while she works."

Martin's hold on his forehead had stilled into more of a vice grip than a massage, as his *mamm* slipped past them in a hurry. With a sigh he dropped his hand, then motioned with an outstretched arm for Cassie to go ahead of him.

"Don't worry, Martin. I have it all figured out. And I have a plan." Maybe not a fully formed one, but it would be by the time they got back.

"Why would I worry?" He gave her a weak smile as he reached around her shoulder to open the cab door. "Ladies first."

Ignoring his sarcasm, she accepted the gentlemanly gesture and slid to the middle of the seat and buckled up. Everything was going to work out. Martin Beiler belonged in Promise, Virginia. And she was going to make sure he came to the same conclusion before these three months ended.

Martin had never been capable of plowing headlong from one situation to the next. For Cassie, decisions came fast and easy. Then, if she regretted her choices, she just made a new plan. Incredibly, that worked for her, as if she had an innate instinct he could never understand.

But Martin needed time to think things through, and he didn't get the luxury of time to consider anything much about moving back to Promise for the summer. He was still reeling from the tornado-like speed of it all. So having Cassie along turned out to be a tremendous help. She'd made quick work of packing up his belongings. He was both amazed and grateful.

Not that he required too many personal belongings, and most of what he owned was related to his work. He wasn't taking all of that with him, only what was necessary and fit into the van of the local fellow he'd hired to drive him and Cassie back to Promise.

Martin had a driver's license. He'd just never gone so far as to purchase a car. Somehow, that always felt like a final break from his past. One he hadn't been ready to make yet. He had considered that if he ever joined the Beachy Amish, he'd get his own work truck that complied with their rules.

Still, something held him back, even though his indecision made his life more complicated. And he couldn't explain his reason for waiting.

So, this afternoon, he was borrowing his uncle's truck to go to a few of the local farms and inspect his hives before he left the bees to the business of making a bountiful honey harvest. The hiccup was finding something for Cassie to do in the meantime. For certain sure, she wouldn't want to tag along to see his bees.

He could drive her back to his uncle's house to visit, but they weren't really her kinfolk. She might be uncomfortable spending the afternoon there.

"Is that everything?" Cassie held open the screen door to the front porch and looked to where they'd stacked the boxes to put in the van later.

His heart skipped a beat, seeing her there on the threshold of his humble bachelor cabin. He shook his head to distract himself from the wayward thought of how he liked having her back in his life again.

"I believe so." He was still at a loss for what to do next, and he needed to hurry up if he was to finish his tasks and get Cass back to Promise tonight.

"We ought to be going to check on those bees of yours, then. I made lunch for us to eat on the way. I'm surprised you didn't starve on the little bit of nothing you had in this kitchen. But at least I used it up and nothing will go to waste…while you're home." She placed a heavy emphasis on the last word.

"*Denki*, Cass, for making lunch." He almost added that this was his home, but thought better of arguing the point.

He was more stuck on the fact she'd said *we ought to be going.* "You don't mind coming along? I thought you'd rather not be around the hives."

She let the door slip shut behind her and stepped across the porch and closer to him. "It's not that I don't mind the bees. It's just that I'm more curious than I am frightened. I'd like to see what you've been doing all this time." Her right hand fretted with the shoulder strap of her apron. "Besides, I can stay in the truck, can't I?"

"*Ya.* Of course, you can." The pleasant feeling of having her in his life resurfaced. And out here, away from the gossip and other folks' expectations, he supposed it couldn't do any harm. They could enjoy the natural goodness of their friendship. He had missed it. Missed her.

"If you're sure…about coming with me—" he felt his cheeks stretch wide from the grin, which he couldn't stop if he tried "—I'd love to show you."

As they climbed back into the truck, Cassie sat beside him with their lunch in a box at her feet to keep it from spilling. He turned the key and set off at a slow speed to reduce the jostling from the rained-out ruts in the gravel drive back to the main road.

Martin knew Eli Weaver was meticulous about his driveway. Cassie's *datt* even kept the farm paths through their fields to feed livestock well maintained. No easy feat in the mountain terrain of Promise.

Truthfully, the bumpy ride of his driveway never bothered him, until this moment when it embarrassed him. And of course, today of all days, the ruts were deeper than ever. "Sorry about that. Must've been a big spring storm last night."

"I've been on country roads before." She gave him a

teasing grin, even though she was holding on to her seat belt as if to save her life.

"The first farm we visit won't be much better. The bee-yard is in a far field halfway up a ridge. Likely, there'll be cattle grazing. That's the main reason I need to go over there—to make sure my fencing is keeping their livestock away from the hives."

She looked over her shoulder to the truck bed behind them. "I wondered what the posthole digger was for."

"When I went to check the bees at the end of the winter, I made a temporary fix to a loose post. I'll have to shore it up before I go. If the cows manage to get to the hives, they'll likely tip them over."

"Won't the bees sting them to protect themselves?"

"For sure, if the hive is threatened, they would. But that may not be enough, and I don't want to take any chances while I'm away. This is one of my best producing beeyards due to all the alfalfa and clover fields nearby."

"And the farmer is Amish?"

"Old Order Mennonite. He's more than happy to have my bees pollinating his crops, and his wife loves the honey I give them in return."

"I see." But she sounded a little puzzled. "So you have a *goot* system going here, then."

He didn't think she'd been asking a question, not exactly, and then her mouth turned down in an almost pout. "That bothers you?"

She shook her head. "*Nay.* I just… Nothing. It's just different than I imagined, is all."

"And that's bad?"

"*Nay.*" She said not, but her frown deepened.

He must be reading her wrong. After all, social cues weren't his specialty, and he must be rusty with Cassie.

Used to be, she was the one person he understood. Letting it go, he focused on the drive.

As he drove through the pasture with his beeyard, he noticed the old post had tipped precariously close to the ground. Still, the barbed wire was intact, and he saw no signs that the hives had been disrupted.

Next to him, Cassie squinted through the windshield. "I might not know anything about bees, but I know how to drive a hole in the ground." Her smile returned as she looked at him. "I might be of some *goot* to you, Martin."

"Some *goot*?" He put the truck in park and applied the emergency brake to keep the vehicle from rolling back down the hillside. "Don't be ridiculous, Cass. Of course, you are."

She was more than some *goot*. And she had to know so.

She rubbed at the tip of her nose and sniffled.

"Cass? *Vass ist letz?*"

"Nothing."

But something was the matter. She wasn't even looking at him. "Listen, you don't have to get out of the truck. I don't expect you to dig holes or come anywhere near the bees. This won't take me long."

She cleared her throat and turned to face him with a smile—false or real he couldn't tell. "It's not the bees. I want to be a help. Truly. Please let me."

They would get done faster and be on their way if she helped. He was still unsure what exactly was wrong with Cassie today, but they may as well get this job underway. He opened his door and walked around to the tailgate where she met him.

That's when he saw her eyes were slightly red.

Martin scratched at the itch that began just above his elbow. She'd been upset the night before, as well. "Are you upset about the bargain I made with your *datt*?"

"I am thankful you agreed to stay and help me." She shrugged. "I just wish you hadn't told him that you'd leave again in three months."

"He doesn't want me to stay, Cass. The only reason he agreed was because I said I'd leave again." He rested his hand on her shoulder, and she looked up at him. How could he make her understand? "I want to help you, too. And this is the best way I know how to…to work things out with your *datt*, so that I can."

She'd figured that out as she'd lain awake last night. But hearing Martin say so felt cold and calculating on her *datt*'s part. And her *datt* wasn't those things. He'd come around. She was sure. As sure as she'd been that she'd also be able to entice Martin out of his horrible reclusive life down here in the valley.

Only his life wasn't so terrible or so lonely, she was discovering today. His cabin might not have had much by way of a stocked pantry, but it was neat as a pin and cozy. He had all these neighboring farmers who happily let him set up his hives on their land. And even their wives loved him for the honey. Not to mention that he also had family here with his uncle and his large brood of children.

The tears she'd been holding back threatened to rise to the surface again. Determined not to make a fool of herself again by crying over him, she looked away from Martin, who waited for her to respond to him.

He'd been all kindness, which made this even harder.

"But that's not all. You don't want to stay in Promise, do you?"

"I can't stay, Cass. My livelihood is here. I have bees all the way up the valley, almost to Winchester. That's how I could afford to lease the farm, so Nick and Fern wouldn't lose it. A few dozen hives in Promise won't make a living wage. So even if your *datt* and the bishop were inclined to welcome me back..." He slumped against the tailgate and looked into the distance. "*Vell*, they aren't, so that's strike two."

"It takes three." She moved beside him and rested a hip against the tailgate. "You're not out, yet, Martin."

He glanced sideways at her, then kicked at a clod of dirt but made no response.

What else could she say? Her *datt*'s behavior of late was a mystery to her, as well. "I truly want you to be happy and be where *Gott* means for you to be. And I can see that you have built a life for yourself here." The admission still stung. "But I don't want you to leave again in three months. I miss you." She glanced back at him and found him watching her with a tenderness in his expression that stole her breath.

A cow lowed in the distance. A chickadee trilled nearby. And her heart drummed in her chest as Martin remained silent for several more beats.

I miss you, too. His eyes said the words, though his lips didn't move.

"I'm sorry," he said instead.

And then, with a determined set of his mouth, he straightened his shoulders, turned and reached for the post-hole digger. Had she imagined the moment of silent communication between them?

"We have to be careful, Cass. I don't want to give folks the wrong idea. Can you imagine how upset my *mamm* will be if she gets her hopes up? I can't stay, and I don't want to hurt people I care about. I can't do that again. Not to my *mamm*. And especially not to you."

Before she could swallow the lump in her throat and answer him, he took a few long strides toward the post that needed to be mended.

"Grab the smoker...just in case," he called over his shoulder and motioned for her to join him.

Why, oh why, did his inclusion of her in the people he cared about have to make her heart pound? It shouldn't when caring about her meant he had to stay away from her. And all because he didn't want to hurt her feelings again. He was clearly determined to serve his three months like a community service sentence and get back out of Promise.

Despite his best intentions, he was wrong. There was absolutely nothing he could do to prevent Cassie's heart from breaking at the end of the summer, if he left.

Or his sweet *mamm*'s.

Like Martin had said, encouraging their families' matchmaking ideas was a bad idea. And now she knew it would run Martin away faster than it would help her convince him to stay.

What had she done? And how was she going to fix it?

If she hadn't been such a ninny three years ago and cried when he left. If she could convince him that she was perfectly content just being friends, maybe he'd change his mind. They'd been the best of friends before. She could be satisfied with that again. She had to. Or he'd never return to Promise.

Chapter Five

The following morning, Martin awoke in an upstairs bedroom of his brother-in-law's former farmhouse—his home for the next three months.

Being at home in Promise again was a strange new reality. But he'd be back down the mountain in his actual home, where he belonged, soon enough. And he needed to keep that in mind. He'd come close to forgetting yesterday.

Time alone with Cassie was dangerous, if he wanted his heart intact when the time came to go. And he hadn't been bluffing about his *mamm*, either. Martin couldn't live with himself if he hurt her again, the way he and Seth had when they left before.

Still, he didn't regret agreeing to help Cassie. She deserved the chance to do what she loved. And, if all went according to plan, the farm would prove beneficial for honey making, too.

Over the next few weeks, he hoped to make quick work of converting the kitchen, dining room and family room into a bakery and storefront, so Cassie could open as soon as possible.

Whether he'd made the agreement with Eli to leave in three months or not, he would have to go in order to harvest his honey. Too bad he hadn't thought to explain that to Cassie yesterday. She could call that strike three.

But he was already out, and he knew it.

He'd struck out with Cassie years ago. And he couldn't help but think of that as his big third strike, when she made the baseball analogy the day before.

From the very beginning, when he decided to bring those hives up to the mountains, he'd known to be careful. Cassie and his *mamm* both wanted him to come back to stay. But in less than twenty-four hours he'd gotten himself tangled up in this scheme of Cassie's that was only bound to leave both his *mamm* and his friend disappointed.

Not to mention how time with Cassie made him wonder what it would be like if he did return. And that kind of thinking would only make it more difficult for all of them when the time came to leave again.

He had to be more careful, especially for Cassie's sake. Her tearful expression yesterday had almost been his undoing. If that was what one called the breathtaking emotion that had engulfed him as she'd looked up at him so sweetly. Whatever it was, he hadn't recognized it as anything to do with how one felt toward a friend.

No *goot* would come of feeling that way toward a woman he couldn't have, and he'd done his best to hide it from her. And he'd do himself no favors recalling it now, either.

He finished dressing and went downstairs to light the stove and put the *kaffi* on.

"It's about time." A feminine voice startled him as he rounded the corner to the kitchen. His sister, Fern, blew out the match she'd used to do the job he'd come down for. Then she turned to him. *"Kaffi?"*

"Ya. I was about to make it." He wasn't too surprised that his sister would sneak into his house, except that she was

married now. "Aren't married women and mothers meant to turn their sisterly ways onto their husbands and children and let their poor younger brothers alone?"

She removed a tea towel from the top of a plate laden with fried eggs, sausage and baked apples. Waving it under his nose, she laughed. "Perhaps I should take this back."

"That would be unusually cruel. I've always said you are the best sister." He lunged for the plate, but she was faster and held it away from him. She was going to make him grovel, and it smelled too *goot* to mind. "Sorry, I didn't mean to be rude. Haven't had my *kaffi*, yet."

With a satisfied grin, she sat the plate down on the table and handed him a fork. "I came to let you know we've found a replacement for Cassie at the store. It will only take a day or two to train her, and then Cassie can put all her energy into getting this place ready to open."

"That's *wunnerbar*. Cassie must be excited." The breakfast in front of him was making his mouth water, and he hoped this conversation wouldn't last too long. He snuck a sausage link into his mouth.

"I haven't told her yet. I thought maybe you'd like to give her the *goot* news."

Was this some sort of matchmaking ploy? He didn't know. Fern's eyebrow was raised like this idea had some hidden meaning. Telling Cassie that she'd been easily replaced didn't sound romantic to him. In fact, he'd rather not. There must be another explanation.

"Why would I want to do that?" He swallowed the sausage. "You and Nick are her employers."

Fern huffed and turned back to making the *kaffi*, seeming to have nothing to say—finally. He bowed his head for a silent prayer over his breakfast before dunking the corner of his toast into the egg yolk.

What promised to be a delicious bite was almost to his mouth when Fern asked, "Aren't you the least bit happy that you will have this time with Cassie?"

Silly question. When had he ever not enjoyed time with Cassie?

He chose a simple nod for an answer and shoved the bite into his mouth before further explanation was required.

Fern propped her hands on her hips. "I'm sure Cassie will be glad to know that she can begin. This is a dream come true for her, you know. I thought you'd like to share the moment with her. As. Her. Friend..." His sister drawled out the word friend with hidden meaning. "I told her to come up here as soon as she got today's bread in the oven. She'll be here any minute."

The bite of his toast lodged sideways in his throat. He coughed it down.

"The *kaffi* should perk soon. I better get back to the store." Her curt tone brought his head up. "You're welcome, *bruder*." Then, his sister was gone in a flash and didn't bother to keep the screen door from slamming on her way out.

Martin had no idea what that was all about. He hadn't even had a chance to properly thank her for his breakfast. He polished off the rest of his breakfast.

Cassie was coming soon and they could get to work.

All would be well. As long as he kept on task and avoided anything that hinted of matchmaking. In three months, Cass would have her bakery and he would be back home where he belonged.

Everything would return to normal. As it was meant to be—like Cassie kept saying—whether or not exactly how she intended.

* * *

Cassie's neck warmed from the sun as she walked up the lane from the store to the farmhouse. Reaching back with her palm, she covered the bare area under her hairline. The skin was still tender from too much sun the day before while working outdoors with Martin.

Today's skies were clear again, and the temperature was already warm. Purple mountain laurel blossoms opened toward the light in the shade of Ada Beiler's front lawn. Such a beautiful morning could only lift her spirits higher.

Cassie waved to Martin's *grossmmami* who sat on her front porch. Her cottage was directly across the lane from the driveway up to Martin's farmhouse. Ada waved back as Cassie turned up the lane to meet Martin.

For most of her life, she'd known this farm as her uncle Nick's place. But for more than a year now, he and Fern had lived in their new house above Weaver's Store. Martin had asked her not to call the farm his, so now she was at a loss for how to refer to it.

She paused a few yards from the steps leading up to the house. With her head tilted slightly, she observed the old place, trying to see it with fresh eyes and a touch of imagination for how it might appear to strangers—tourists on their way through the Blue Ridge.

Martin ambled toward her from the side entrance to the kitchen. His hands were in his pockets. He hadn't bothered to put his hat over a mess of uncombed hair, but he wore a smile. He always remained handsome regardless of the rumpled state he favored when he was alone.

"What should we call it?" She nodded toward the gabled front porch, where she imagined a sign might hang.

"Whatever *you* want to call it. It's your bakery, Cass."

"Well, whatever I name it, *we* will all be calling it by

that name." She gave him a teasing glare. "Including you, mister smarty-pants."

His grin widened as he came to stand beside her and survey the house as she had been doing. "Are you asking for my opinion on a name?"

"Duh." She bumped his shoulder with her own. "Weaver's Bakery seems redundant, since we already have Weaver's Amish Store. Besides, I don't expect to be a Weaver forever."

Martin's posture stiffened, and he remained silent.

"No ideas?" She was a tad disappointed. She'd hoped he might have a genius idea up his sleeve.

But then he scratched at his elbow before rubbing the back of his neck. "What about Cassie's Country Bakehouse?"

He stepped forward, held his arms up toward the house and spread them wide as if outlining a sign. "I can see it. What do you think?" He turned around to face her. "Unless you're also hoping to change your first name to something different than Cassie, then that won't work."

He was joking, of course, but oh, my…that look in his eyes. The green darkened and seared into her with some question she hadn't heard him ask. Because he surely knew she wasn't going to change her given name.

Her name. She'd referenced her married name, whatever that might one day be. Her heart stuttered to a stop. "*Nay*, Martin. No one is offering to change my name."

Indeed, there were no secret courtships in her life. Not with Martin. Not with anyone.

"*Goot.*" Martin didn't often maintain eye contact as long as he did just then, before he blew out a little breath and looked away again. "So, what about Cassie's Country Bakehouse?"

"I like it. Very much." Unsure where the sudden tension had come from, she released a breath of her own before responding. "I knew you'd have a *wunnerbar goot* idea."

They'd reached an awkward standstill. Neither spoke nor moved. And Cassie had to wonder if his mind was as much on the idea of a secret courtship as hers had become all of a sudden.

She opened her mouth to ask, but the words got stuck. How exactly did one go about asking a man if he'd consider trying out a secret courtship? *Hey, since everyone already thinks we're courting behind their backs, why don't we give it a whirl and see what happens?*

Her cheeks flamed at the thought.

Then Martin spoke before she had the nerve.

"Kumm." He strode away, calling to her over his shoulder as he headed toward the house. "I need you to show me what to do."

Of course, Martin hadn't been contemplating the idea of a courtship with her. Hadn't she learned her lesson yesterday? She was a *dummkopf* and needed to rein in her imagination. She couldn't allow a wish for what might never be with Martin to ruin the blessings *Gott* was giving her now.

She quickly caught up with him and followed behind because he was right. There was a great deal to be done to make Cassie's Country Bakehouse a reality. Opening a new business was a big undertaking. Uncle Nick believed in her, and Martin did, too. He wouldn't be helping her otherwise.

Maybe Martin didn't need her as much as she'd hoped. But she needed him. And she sure wasn't ready to give up on convincing him to stay in Promise.

She only had to figure out how to keep all notions of anything more than friendship with him far—very far— out of her thoughts. Focusing on all the work ahead of her seemed as sensible a way as any. The busier she stayed, the less time there'd be for ideas of a secret courtship with Martin Beiler.

Martin held the front door open for her. "Where would you like to begin? Here? Or in the kitchen?"

This was the easy part. She'd been dreaming up how to make this house work for months. She stepped into the living room. "We just walked through the main entrance. I want the customers to come in through the porch, so we might need to add a ramp at the end to make it wheelchair accessible and make this a double door. Do you think that's possible?"

"I'm a decent enough carpenter from all *Datt* taught me growing up, but I'd like his advice on the best way to add a ramp. He'll know all the codes we have to follow and such." He examined the doorway and knocked on the walls on both sides. "I don't think widening this door will be an issue." He turned to face Cassie. His brow raised. "Next?"

She walked farther into the room and stretched her arms out wide. "This room will be the main part of the store, where customers will shop and purchase goods." She nodded in his direction. "There, by the door, will be the checkout counter. And we can put shelving along the walls and even an island or two in the middle of the room for displays."

Martin walked around the perimeter of the room, then looked up at the ceiling. "A fresh coat of paint might be a *goot* idea before we add shelves. What about the floor?"

She hadn't thought about the flooring. "Is there a problem with having wood floors?"

"*Nay*, I just wanted to make sure that's what you want." He smiled at her. "Although a *goot* landlord would probably give them a fresh buff and shine with a fresh coat of stain and shellac. Do you have a decent landlord?"

She shrugged her shoulders and tried not to smile. "I reckon I'm about to find out."

He tilted his head back and laughed.

"What next?"

"*Vell*, this doorway to the kitchen would be better if it were widened, so I can see out into the store. I won't always have help and will need to keep watch for customers."

Martin studied the wall from both sides. "Do you want the entire wall to come down?"

She shook her head. "I don't think so. I'd lose too much cabinet space in the kitchen."

"Sounds simple enough, then. And in the kitchen?" He walked through the door and waited for her to join him. "Do you need more cabinets?"

"*Ya*, but I haven't figured out where they will go. I will need another oven, too, and that will take up space, even though I can't afford to add it just yet."

"I'm sure we can find a solution. This other stuff is more *Datt*'s specialty, you know. I'm much better at cabinets and such. Between us all, we can make it work just how you want it to."

Construction and cabinet making were the jobs that took Seth and Martin away from Promise. She had no doubt in his ability, along with his father's, to do a *wunnerbar* job.

A happy memory of a young eager Martin showing her his handiwork came to mind. She'd been visiting her grandparents, and he'd come from his home next door to find her. "I remember when you made your first ten frame for the bees. You were so thrilled."

"*Ya*, I was." He leaned against the counter and smiled. "*Datt* was an amazing carpenter, and Seth could already do almost anything our *datt* asked him to do." Martin pointed to himself and shrugged. "It wasn't so easy for me. So, it was a smart idea, really, for *Datt* to encourage me by teaching me on the basic beehive. Though it took me longer than most kids my age, it was simple enough for me to master eventually, and because I wanted to work with the bees more than the construction business, I was motivated."

"You have a *goot datt, ya*?"

"We are blessed, for sure, in having fathers who love us. Eli also only wants what is best for you." He sighed and scratched at his elbow. Martin always got nervous at the mention of her *datt*, so she found it especially kind that he included him in the good father category. "I suppose I better get to work, so you can open. The sooner the better, right? Fern says they found a baker to work at the store."

She nodded. "Ruby Yoder came in this morning. She is getting on up in years, you know, so she doesn't want a full-time job. But she agreed to fill in temporarily."

"What then? I mean, I suppose they'll find someone else soon enough."

"Uncle Nick says that once I get my bakery up and running, he'll keep a standing order with me to keep all of his baked goods stocked."

"That's *wunnerbar*, Cass. You'll have a steady stream of income from the very start." He looked around the room. "I best find my tools and get started. I think I saw a tape measure in that drawer." He pointed to the one next to her.

She rummaged through what must have been her uncle's catch-all junk drawer. He'd left it all behind. "Here's one."

"That will work." He took the tape measure in a hurry. "The sooner I get started, the better, right?"

"Right," she answered weakly as his quick strides carried him out of sight.

Her dream was coming true, and having Martin's eager help should make her happy. She tried to push out the feeling that he was more in a rush to get away from her than excited about getting her bakery opened.

The mention of her *datt* had changed his mood. For a little while, she'd been sure Martin was feeling comfortable and at home—exactly what he needed to feel, if he was ever going to decide to stay. But all of a sudden, he seemed itching to get this job over so he could be on his way.

And all because he'd felt compelled to promise her *datt* that he'd leave.

Ach! She opened the cabinet under the sink and grabbed a roll of steel wool. She needed to clean something, even if the kitchen was already spotless.

Martin couldn't believe how fast his thoughts toward Cassie had spiraled out of the friend zone. How could he help it, though? The thought of her name ever changing from Weaver to anything else—anything other than Beiler—was maddening.

Who could possibly take care of her, understand her, treat her the way she deserved? He didn't know of another a man who knew her the way he did. And he couldn't imagine one worthy of a woman like Cass.

And there was the rub.

He wasn't that worthy of a man, either.

Looking around for a task—preferably one requiring a hammer and some nails to pound—he stopped when someone called his name.

"Martin?" a male voice called. "Cassie?"

"In here, Zach," Cassie answered from the kitchen, and Martin headed that way to greet her brother.

"What are you doing here?" she asked her younger sibling, who towered above her. He was seventeen and the spitting image of his father.

"Why do you think? *Datt* sent me to chaperone." Zach's eyes rolled, then he spotted Martin leaning against the doorway. "Sorry, Martin, no offense."

"None taken." Martin nodded at Zach. "*Goot* to see you."

"Speak for yourself," Cassie muttered and gave her brother a playful jab on the arm.

"Don't worry. I won't be breathing down your necks. Besides, as your *bruder*, I ought to be helping you with this project." Zach glanced between them.

"There's enough work to go around." Martin moved farther into the room. "Cassie has a clear vision of what she wants already. Most of what needs to be done to begin is basic carpentry work…building some shelves, widening doorways." Martin motioned toward the one he'd just come through. "At some point we'll paint and redo the floors. But for now, I'm still sizing up the job."

"*Datt* mentioned something about converting a storage shed out back for a cooling system to store bulk products. Keep the need for electricity out of the house and all that."

"Hold on, now." Cassie stepped between them. "Maybe later. I can't afford it yet. And there's no guarantee I'll do enough business to require one." There was an edge to her voice.

Zach winked at his sister. "But it gives me a reason to stay out of your way."

Martin always had liked Zach. Although, feeling appreciative of his matchmaking didn't make sense. Martin should be discouraging folks from believing there was something between him and Cassie.

She gave a delicate snort at her brother's suggestion.

"Martin might need your help to build those shelves."

She sure didn't sound as keen on being alone with Martin as her brother seemed to believe she would be.

And why was he disappointed?

"As I said, I don't want to make a nuisance of myself." Zach was already easing his way out of the kitchen by way of the mudroom to the back door. "You know where to find me, if you need me."

Martin truly didn't mind Zach being around to help. He appreciated it, despite the weird disappointment he'd felt a moment earlier.

Still, Eli didn't trust him enough to work alone with his daughter, and that irritated him like the rub of a burr caught in his clothing. And he couldn't make out for sure what Cassie thought of being chaperoned.

Annoyed. *Nay*, not exactly. The color in her cheeks had brightened. Embarrassed, maybe.

He touched her shoulder to reassure her. "Don't worry, I won't be indulging in this secret wooing your brother imagines is going on when he's not looking."

She didn't meet his gaze, which meant something different from when he was too uncomfortable to look someone in the eye. Usually, it meant she was embarrassed.

"As if..." she muttered to herself.

"*Vass?* As if...what?"

"As if you'd ever do anything so romantic. As if I could ever expect any man to be that way with me. *Datt* would frighten off anyone that tried. Not that you *ever* would." She waved a ball of steel wool in one hand and propped the other firmly on her hip. "Try. Not that you would try."

Cassie's mood could change on a dime like that. He struggled to keep up. Did she want him to woo her?

"Is that a challenge?"

"*Nay.*" Her rebuttal came without any hesitation, then

she looked upward as though praying for help. "*Nay*. I am not up for any wooing or secret courtships or any other matchmaking scheme."

If only she knew how much he'd considered doing exactly that not an hour ago. But Eli Weaver had made his opinion of Martin as clear as possible. As if—in Cassie's words—he wasn't already aware.

"Besides, who wants or needs the hassle of the minister's daughter?" she huffed.

He wasn't sure she'd meant for him to hear that, or if she'd even intended to say it aloud by the way she froze and clamped her mouth tightly closed.

Eli Weaver was a formidable force to any man with an interest in his daughter. Truth be told, Martin had always feared him a little. Sometimes, a lot. And apparently Martin wasn't the only one who'd been intimidated by the prospect of wooing the minister's daughter.

For the second time that morning, the thought of any other suitor for Cassie made his stomach sour.

Could he woo Cassie? Would she have him if he tried? Martin rubbed at his temples.

"Cass… I—"

She held up the scrub-brush-wielding hand. "*Bitte*, Martin…we don't need to talk about it. I've had enough humiliation for a morning. And so have you, probably. I shouldn't be surprised that *Datt* would interfere, and I apologize if it seems an insult to you." Her shoulders slumped and her hands dropped loosely at her sides. "All I want is for us to be friends…the way we used to be."

No matter how well he knew that friendship was all he'd ever have with her, he couldn't say he liked her stating it so clearly.

"Don't worry about it anymore. I won't encourage the matchmakers anymore. I know it upset you. I wish we could just start over from the morning you arrived with your bees."

He wouldn't mind a do-over himself. He wasn't the least bit happy with the way things stood between them right now. "And what would you change?"

"I wouldn't manipulate you into staying, Martin. That's not what I want. As much as I want you to be here…to have my friend back… I want you to want it, too."

"I don't regret agreeing to stay, Cass. You didn't force me into it. I want to help you."

"For three months."

She was a stubborn woman. "I explained that."

"My *datt*, I know."

"And my work, Cass. I have to make a living." He stepped closer to her in case Zach was within hearing distance. "You know, it's complicated. Since I left before being baptized into the church, that might mean I'm not shunned. But you know as well as I do, I'm not fully welcome, either."

Her eyes widened, as if his words pained her. It was a hard truth he'd come to accept. He didn't relish reminding her of it, but she seemed determined to ignore the obvious.

She looked down at her hands now wringing the steel wool. He took the abrasive from her and tossed it in the sink before she ruined her hands. She looked up at him. "What if it were different?"

He shook his head.

What did it matter? Things were the way they were.

"I see," she said before turning her back to him and facing the sink.

They'd reached an impasse. Some space would do them

both good. "I'll head down to the hardware store to get some supplies, assuming Zach brought your *datt*'s wagon."

She glanced out the window. "*Ya*, he did."

"I'll take your *bruder* with me." Martin waited for her response, which came as a simple nod before he went out the way Zach had a few minutes prior.

Zach appeared around the corner, as though sent to remind Martin that he'd given Eli his word that he'd leave in three months. And more to the point, any attempt at courting Cassie was out of the question.

"Lover's spat?" Zach wiggled his eyebrows. Not a *goot* look, even if it seemed to work in the kid's favor with the girls.

"Hmm," Martin grunted. "We need to go get some lumber."

Offering no more explanation, Martin walked toward the wagon. Zach took the hint and followed.

None of this courting business was in the bargain, not the one he'd made with Cassie or the one with her father. And for sure and certain, he hadn't come to Promise to woo Cassie Weaver. All he intended to do was set up a few beehives and leave, letting the industrious little creatures do their job until he came back to harvest their honey and make a tidy profit.

But other people's ideas that he had additional intentions were complicating everything. Maybe even ruining a friendship he was finding more important to him than ever.

Cassie was right. Martin had no clue how to be romantic, even if courting her wouldn't endanger the shaky approval he had from her *datt* to help her start her business.

Still, she was his friend, the best he'd ever had. Maybe he fell short in the romance category, but he could be a better friend. And he could build her a kitchen island to solve her need for an extra oven and more cabinet space.

Ya, that he could do.

And it would be the best kitchen island in all of Virginia.

Chapter Six

The month of April had been exhausting. Now, on the first of May, Cassie walked from the store up the hill to the renovations of the farmhouse, soon to be her new bakery, and every muscle from the bottom of her chin to the tops of her toes ached.

But when she noticed the lawn now cleared of all the debris that had accumulated as walls and doors and porch flooring had been ripped up, the pain was worth the long hours of the previous days and weeks.

With a squint she tried to picture a grand opening banner alongside a new sign above the porch. Now that the place looked less like a construction site, she could see her dream coming true. Cassie's Country Bakehouse was becoming a reality.

She placed her palms against her lower back and stretched a tightening muscle. But they weren't done yet. If all went well, though, the grand opening would be possible after Ascension Day in the middle of the month but before Memorial Day at the end.

Martin and Zach had gone straight to Burkholder's this morning to pick up wood stain and the extra flooring they'd ordered to fill the gaps where the doors had been expanded.

She entered the house through the side door to the

kitchen and noticed right off that the sawdust and wood chippings from yesterday's work had already been cleaned and the floor mopped. Sometimes kindness worked better than a pain reliever. She actually felt her sore muscles relax. And it wasn't the first time Martin had surprised her with a simple but thoughtful act like that over the past few weeks.

Spinning in a slow circle, she examined the full view of the kitchen. The widened doorway gave her a perfect open view of the living room just as she'd hoped. Cassie's Country Bakehouse ought to give her customers a down-home feel, but nevertheless she'd maintain it as an efficient business.

The simple home kitchen that had been in her uncle's home for decades was a great start and would work just fine with a few improvements. She didn't need fancy equipment, but selling in the quantities she hoped for would eventually require more work space and a second oven. For now, she must be thankful for what she had.

So far, over the past weeks of renovation, her resolve to remain busy and focused on the task at hand had been a huge success. Not once had she made a fool of herself over Martin. And every time he did something extra thoughtful or super sweet, she managed to remind herself that he only did so as a friend.

So far, so *goot*. Martin even seemed to enjoy working alongside her. Her *datt* hadn't interfered other than to send Zach over at every opportunity. And Martin hadn't mentioned leaving Promise at all.

Ya, these were all very *goot* signs, and her weariness lifted almost completely. Only since Martin had already cleaned, she wasn't sure where to begin before he and Zach returned from the hardware store.

A knock drew her attention to the front door that would

soon be the entrance for customers. She imagined the tinkle of a bell with the door opening and made a mental note to add the addition of one to Martin's to-do list.

Another knock.

Odd. Was it an *Englisher*? Around here, most Amish would just holler and come in. Certainly, her family would. Suddenly she was a little nervous about being alone.

She hadn't even given a thought to locking the doors. No one around here did that, either. She hesitated. Perhaps, her *datt* hadn't been too off the mark in his concern over her being all alone.

"It's me, Reuben Bender. I was looking for Martin." A decidedly masculine voice called out from the other side of the door. "I don't mean to frighten you. Don't worry, I'll not be coming in."

Relief washed through her. She was being silly. An intruder wouldn't have knocked. And Reuben Bender was Amish. While his size surely might intimidate almost anyone, Cassie had no reason to fear him. He was simply strong, as *Gott* had made him to be. She was aware other girls gossiped about him and shied away from him because of some mysterious past. Those rumors had followed him ever since he came to Promise a few years ago.

She didn't know the details because she'd refused to listen to the gossip.

The creak of the wooden steps alerted her that Reuben had decided to leave.

She rushed to door and swung it open. "Reuben, wait!"

What could she say? That she hadn't been frightened—that would be a lie. But she hadn't been afraid for the reason he must have assumed, that she wanted to avoid him like the other girls did.

Skipping an explanation, she smiled in the friendliest

way she knew how. "Martin and Zach have gone for supplies. I'm sure they'll be back shortly."

He paused at the bottom of the steps and looked up at her. "There's a huge swarm of bees in my woods. I thought Martin might want to come get them."

She shuddered involuntarily at the mention of bees and swarms. Hideous things.

Reuben looked down at the grass. "If you would, let him know for me, then I'll be going."

Oh, dear. He still thought he frightened her.

"You can wait here, if you'd like." She motioned to the chairs on the front porch. "I don't have anything to offer but a cool glass of sweet tea."

A touch of surprise flickered across his face. "*Denki.* That is a kind gesture. But I better be on my way. Just let him know that he's welcome to capture those bees for his honey making. He can even leave them on my land, if he wants."

"I'll be sure to tell him." And keeping the bees on Reuben Bender's property sounded like a fine idea to her. "That's very generous of you."

"Nothing generous. Their *Gott*'s creatures, not mine." He nodded at her. "I appreciate you passing the message along."

"You're welcome," she called back as he'd already turned to go. "But it looks like you can tell him yourself. I believe that's them coming up the lane now."

Sure enough, Martin and Zach could be seen in the distance with a wagonload of timber. However, Reuben didn't wait on the porch. He mounted his horse and rode down the lane to meet them.

Not only would Martin be kind to Reuben, he'd be thrilled about the bees. Indeed, even from a distance his interaction with the man appeared happily animated. She had to smile.

Maybe Martin's delight would make up for her unintended insult to the man.

She hoped so.

And it was just one more reason Martin needed to stay in Promise. Without him, she might have fretted for days that she'd caused Reuben offense. But Martin's nature balanced hers. Surely now, Reuben would feel the kind of welcome and gratitude he deserved for thinking of Martin and his bees.

She'd been doing her best to emphasize to Martin all the ways that Promise was a better place with him in it, ever since he'd told her that he wouldn't be welcomed back. She didn't believe that for a minute. And if her *datt* didn't send Martin any more signals to the contrary, maybe he'd realize so himself.

Reuben had been welcomed into their fellowship despite a regretful past, and he'd flaunted the *Ordnung* far more than Martin had done. That part was fact. She knew because Reuben confessed to the whole church and repented.

Reuben hadn't been accepted as warmly as he might have been. She couldn't deny so. Her own friend Nan Burkholder was much to blame for that. And she suspected Nan regretted her gossip. Reuben was powerful handsome, and she'd seen how Nan looked at him when no one else noticed.

So maybe Promise wasn't perfect. They could do better, she was willing to admit so. But Martin was wrong that he would not be welcomed—and warmly—if he decided to join their church.

Everyone loved Martin. They always had. And why wouldn't they? It was far too hard not to.

Tired and a fraction disappointed, Martin left Reuben Bender's place unsure whether the swarm of honeybees would eventually relocate into the hive he'd set up for them or not. He'd return in the morning to check, but for now he was already late to supper, and he didn't intend to disappoint his *mamm*, as well.

He was also going to ask his *datt* about borrowing a horse. He needed a way to travel around these parts other than on foot. His parents' farm was less than a mile away, but right about now, he'd be tempted to sell his birthright to his twin brother—or his uncle, in this case—for the use of his truck. Hungry and irritated by a half dozen or more stings, a mile seemed a long walk for a pot of stew.

Those wild mountain bees had been more aggressive than he expected. They'd likely settle down soon. And, if *Gott* was willing, the queen bee would take a liking to Martin's box and settle that fractious brood into it overnight. If so, he'd be well on his way to making a profit from mountain honey. The notion lightened his step.

After all, his original purpose had been to make a go of producing mountain honey for his business. Plus, Reuben had been keen to let Martin set up as many as a dozen hives on his property near his lavender fields. It was a win-win for both men, if the bees cooperated.

At first he'd thought nothing could go right after stepping foot back in Promise. But now he and Cassie were making good progress on her bakery and his honey-making endeavors might pay off better than he hoped.

Sensibly, he ought to have begun his business here where his love of bees started in the first place. But he'd avoided his hometown ever since he left three years ago. Granted, he hadn't made the break from family and faith as hard as his twin brother, Seth, had done.

As much as any other reason, Martin had left with Seth to try and keep his *bruder* out of too much trouble. He hadn't succeeded. And now, he had no idea of Seth's whereabouts, only that he headed to Florida.

No one asked about Seth anymore. It hurt too much.

Saying his name was all that was necessary to melt his *mamm* into a puddle of tears. He knew that his family prayed fervently over his brother, just as he did every single day. Still, they rarely spoke of him.

At first, Martin had avoided Promise for Seth's sake. Seth would threaten to disappear altogether at any hint of a visit back home. After about a year, he made good on that threat, anyway. And then, Martin avoided home to dodge all the questions about Seth and his whereabouts—and worse, Martin's failure to be his brother's keeper. Only when he'd been in a position to help his sister, Fern, had he found returning to Promise worth the effort.

After that it only made sense to expand his business back up to the mountains where the beekeeping idea really began. And now, Cassie needed his help, and he found himself slowly forgetting all the reasons he and Seth had found to leave in the first place.

He'd always followed Seth's lead. Had the ideas ever been his own or had it been Seth's discontent spilling over?

Not only had they looked nothing alike, Seth was also Martin's opposite in every way possible. He knew what to say in any situation. He knew how to make friends. He knew how to get a girl to fall in love with him at first sight. Seth seemed to know everything, and Martin hadn't known how to navigate life without his brother.

Until he had to.

And somehow, with *Gott*'s favor, he'd managed.

He'd focused on the one thing he was good at on his own—keeping bees. Somehow, he'd managed to earn the respect and trust of his neighbors. His cabin was comfortable, and no one around minded that he spent his time alone.

Martin was fairly confident that a man like him couldn't expect much more.

So why torture himself with thoughts of having Cassie by his side? For the umpteenth time that day, he pushed aside a mental image of how it would be to come home from collecting honey to the scents of her bakery and the thrill of her smile.

Ya, now he began to remember why he'd been willing to leave—*nay*, run away from Promise. It had been the agonizing reminders of what he would never have that pushed him into joining his brother. And now, he was living it all over again.

Only his cabin down in the valley was beginning to feel less like a quiet sanctuary he wanted to return to and more like a sad, solitary future. And the past month with Cassie hadn't been torture. He looked forward to her arrival each morning and was sorry to see her go at the end of the day.

Maybe this was one more instance in which his brother's advice had been way off the mark. And, maybe friendship with Cassie was worth the risk of never having more.

"I'll be right there," Cassie hollered out the kitchen window to her brother, who was anxious to get going.

They were both expected at their *Grossmammi* Weaver's house for supper.

Quickly, she pulled open a drawer where she'd noticed odds and ends still tucked away from when her uncle lived in the house. Digging through the junk, she found a pencil stub and an unused envelope. She jotted down a short list of reminders to herself, tucked the note in her apron pocket and then replaced the pencil into the drawer.

Satisfied she'd accomplished all she could for the day and knowing she wouldn't be back until the day after next, she slipped out the side door to leave with Zach. About a half mile from her grandparents' house, she caught sight of a man walking along the roadside. His back was to them, as he was headed in the same direction, but he was too familiar not to recognize even at a distance.

"Slow down, Zach. It's Martin."

Her brother pulled back on the reins, slowing to a stop as they reached Martin. He stepped back a few feet to make room for the wagon to pull partway off the side of the road.

"You're going my way, I reckon." He needn't ask, as he knew where they were headed, and the Beiler farm neighbored their grandparents'. Martin's eye caught Cassie's with a bit of a spark, and his lips turned up. "I appreciate you stopping."

"Ach!" her brother grunted and gripped his hand as though pained. "Seems you showed up just in time. My hands are sore from all that sawing. I don't suppose you'd mind taking the reins." Zach hardly waited for an answer before passing Cassie the lead and jumping down to go sit in the wagon bed.

Martin shot her a knowing look as he climbed onto the bench beside her. "What do you suppose is in it for him to keep playing matchmaker?"

"I heard that," Zach called from behind them. "I am mortified to know you don't believe I've worked hard enough today to tire my hands."

Cassie snorted. Fortunately, Martin's simultaneous laugh covered the unladylike sound. She handed him the reins. She was perfectly capable of driving the horse but didn't like to do so from the side where she sat—not on a public road.

Martin wrapped the leads around his palms, then slid to the center of the bench seat.

She could have done the same but hadn't had the boldness. He was so close now. Much closer than normal for a friend.

"I also still have eyes from back here, too," Zach teased, to Cassie's mortification, but Martin made no effort to return to his side of the seat.

"And you'd be safer to turn the other way before I start down the road." Martin flicked the reins. And her brother chuckled as he turned around and sat securely with his back to them.

Cassie's heart drummed in her chest. Was Martin encouraging Zach's mistaken notion that they were courting?

Of course not. She was reading far too much into Martin's actions. Cassie silently recited the well-rehearsed reminder to herself. She ought to know by now that he had no idea how he affected her.

A wagon wheel hit a small hole and the jolt bumped her closer to him. She ought to move back over, only she rather liked where she was. And if Martin noticed, he wasn't giving any indication that he minded how close they sat, either.

If anything, he seemed to relax, although he kept his eyes steady on the road. "Were you satisfied with what you got done after I left?"

"*Ya*, it was a productive day. Mostly, it just revealed all the work that needs to be done." She pulled the list from her pocket. "Since no one will be working tomorrow, I made a list to help me remember everything."

"Smart." He nodded. "Anything on there for me to do?"

"Of course." She bumped his shoulder with hers, careful not to disrupt his driving.

"Is it all for me?"

"Perhaps...mostly." She watched his mouth turn up in a grin at her admission, just as a breeze caught the slip of paper between her fingers like the loose end of a sail. Before she could tighten her grip, it fluttered and twisted out of her hand. She failed to catch it, grasping for the paper as the wind whisked it beyond her reach.

A strong arm steadied her. "You're going to fall out, if you're not careful."

She hadn't paid attention to how far she leaned over the side of the wagon bench. Looking down now made her dizzy. Martin's steady hand around her waist pulled her back safely to her seat.

"Trying to get us all killed?" her brother chastised from behind them. "I doubt there's anything on that paper worth life and limb."

"Leave her be." Martin grunted and returned his focus to maintaining control of the wagon, but he did appear a few shades paler than usual.

Shame flooded her own face with heat. "*Ich bin* sorry."

"*Es shatt nix.*" No harm done. Martin was forgiving. But her brother was right—she might have caused a wreck.

She shuddered, knowing how terrible such an accident could be.

"*Kumm.*" Martin pulled her back closer to him. "I mean it. All is well, so think no more about it, *ya*?"

"*Ya,*" she agreed easily.

Only, she had a feeling her thoughts were going to remain full of remembering the *wunnerbar goot* experience of Martin's protective arm around her and the sweetness of his comforting words.

She couldn't allow herself the luxury of such thinking, though. After all, she knew where it would lead—down a dead-end road—because Martin never intended for them to be anything more than friends. And if Martin would only be around for a couple more months—another thought she couldn't bear—then she mustn't waste the precious moments of friendship they shared.

Once they'd arrived, Martin helped her down. They were to part ways now. He'd go to his parents' house next door and she'd join her family inside of her grandparents' house for supper. But he didn't hurry to leave her. Instead he leaned against the wooden slats on the back of the wagon and propped one heel over the top of his other foot, clearly comfortable.

"We've got about two weeks before Ascension Day and then a couple after that before Memorial Day. So I was thinking, we might easily have everything ready by then for you to open."

"Do you think so?" Her mind whirled with the possibility of opening in time for all the tourists who came through for the start of the summer season.

"I do. We can finish the floors and all the painting in the first two weeks, then Zach and I can add the shelving and complete the ramped entryway the following two weeks. We can make it work…if it will work for you."

"*Ya*, Martin, I can make that work." She'd have lots of baking to do with only one oven, but she'd make it happen. "How *wunnerbar*! *Denki*, for…for everything."

He pushed away from the wagon. "It's my pleasure, Cass."

She watched him go before slowly turning in the opposite direction to join her family.

A friend like Martin was a rare treasure. She'd be wise to enjoy what she had rather than pine for what would never be. She only wished her heart wouldn't make keeping her new resolution so difficult.

Chapter Seven

The evening after Martin, Zach and Cassie painted the inside of the house, a heavy rain began and didn't stop for three days. Finally, the sun shone through the clouds, allowing Cassie to open up the windows and doors so the walls could fully dry and the chemical smell from the painted walls and wood-stained floors could dissipate.

The strong odor had forced Martin to retreat to his parents' house, and Cassie had helped Fern and Ruby at her uncle's store while there was little work she could do on her own bakery. Thankfully, this afternoon, she'd been able to come and open up the house.

She lifted the window of one of the upstairs bedrooms, which left only Martin's bedroom undone. She hadn't wanted to invade his privacy by entering his room. But as she passed by, she realized he wouldn't be able to sleep in the room unless it was aired out.

"Cassie, are you here?" a female voice she recognized as belonging to her friend Nan called from downstairs.

"I'll be right down, Nan," she called back and quickly opened Martin's door. All she'd do was lift his window, not nose around in his things. Surely, he wouldn't mind. After all, she'd helped him pack all his possessions from his cabin for his stay here.

As she turned to go, a breeze scattered the belongings on his bedside stand. She righted an empty tin cup and closed the fluttering pages of the open Bible, when something metallic clattered on the floor.

An old pocket watch lay half-open on the floor, and she bent to retrieve it.

"What's that?" Nan's voice startled her, as if she was doing something very wrong. Her willowy blonde friend stood in the doorway eyeing the object in Cassie's hand. Her bright blue eyes were wide, and her pert nose wrinkled. "Are you snooping?"

"*Nay.* I am not."

Cassie spun around to set the watch down but not before she noticed a locket of hair taped to the inside of the lid. The curl, tied with a single thread of red cotton, was most certainly her own. She sucked in a breath and snapped the watch shut before dropping it beside the Bible.

She tried to still the questions racing through her mind as she turned back to face Nan.

"Hmm. If you say so." One of Nan's eyebrows raised in suspicion as Cassie ushered her into the hallway and back downstairs as fast as possible.

Cassie felt badly enough for going into Martin's room. If he found Nan in there, he'd certainly feel as if she'd breached his trust. And now, she was about to be bombarded with questions, if she knew Nancy-Anne Burkholder at all,

"Why are you blushing, Cassie? If that was nothing you held, and you weren't snooping, then you wouldn't be so pink in the cheeks."

"*Vell.*" Cassie strained for an answer that wasn't an untruth. "The house has been shut up for days. It's overly warm and humid in here. I was simply opening the windows and picked up an old watch that accidentally fell on the floor."

All perfectly true. Though probably not enough to satisfy Nan. She was like a hunting dog on the scent of a squirrel when she latched on to a hint of a gossipy tidbit. Cassie loved her friend, but this one thing drove her mad.

Her friend's mouth turned up in a slow, easy smile.

"Don't even, Nan." She could see the mischief at play on Nan's face. "So, what brings you over?"

Nan gave a small pout but thankfully let the subject drop. "I'd like to help you with your grand opening, and I'm not the only one who'd be willing to volunteer. If you'd like, I can organize several of our church women to be there for the opening. And I will do whatever you need to get ready in the meantime."

As always, Cassie couldn't hold Nan's gossipy nature against her for long. She was too full of other *goot* qualities and always ready to jump in to help in a time of need.

"For sure, Nan, no one could organize a better grand opening than you. I'd love to have your help." She smiled at her friend, truly grateful.

Nan gave a delighted squeal and hugged Cassie around the shoulders. "This will be the most exciting event in Promise for the whole year." She gave Cassie a saucy grin. "Unless someone finally decides to get married."

"I'm warning you, Nan. None of that nonsense. You'll ruin everything."

"So there is something going on…"

"*Nay*, there is not. And if you spread more rumors, it will probably just send Martin running back down the mountain even sooner."

"Oh, Cassie, that is not true. That man adores you. Can't you see it?"

"That is just the problem, Nan. I am doing my best not to read more into the sweet things he does. And it's hard enough without you encouraging me."

"You're being ridiculous." Nan's eyebrows pinched together and her head tilted. "Don't you still like him? You always did before. What you need to do is encourage Martin."

"Encourage me to do what?" The male voice startled them both.

Cassie's heart plummeted to her knees as Martin rounded the corner from the mudroom. The whole purpose for this new open floor plan was to keep anyone from sneaking up on her. Nan had distracted her completely.

As Martin strode across the kitchen toward where they stood in the front room, Cassie sent Nan a glare intended to silence her, no matter how unlikely such a thing might be.

"Nan came by to offer help with the grand opening of the bakehouse." Cassie prayed silently for the change of subject to go unnoticed. "And I opened up all the windows to air out the place."

"*Denki.* I was about to do the same." Martin took a deep breath. "I can tell a difference already."

Nan sent her a sideways grin. "Yep. *All* of the windows are open."

Cassie's face warmed with another blush at the reminder of the locket of her hair in Martin's pocket watch. She wished she could pinch Nan or, better yet, send her on her way.

Thankfully, Martin didn't seem to notice. "The break in the rain gave me a chance to bring some of the shelves I've been working on. Reuben came with me to haul them inside." He looked between Cassie and her friend. "I kinda hoped to surprise you. I didn't expect to find anyone here."

"Oh! A surprise. How *wunnerbar.*" Nan's syrupy sweet

voice was punctuated with a raising of her eyebrows at Cassie. "Such a *friendly* thing to do."

Ignoring the sarcasm and insinuations, Cassie looked beyond Martin. "Where is Reuben?"

"He preferred to wait outside until Nan left."

"Me?" Nan appeared genuinely taken aback. "The surprise is for Cassie."

Cassie blew out a breath. She knew exactly why Reuben wouldn't come inside as long as Nan was there. Could Nan really be so oblivious to how her gossip hurt other people? And Martin, bless him, was as forthright as always. If Reuben didn't want to come inside because of Nan, then Martin just accepted it.

"Let's go down to the store, Nan. We can sit in Fern and Nick's sunroom and talk over the grand opening plans while Martin and Reuben unload the surprise." *Blessed are the peacemakers.* At least, Cassie hoped that's what she was being.

"You will come back, won't you?" Martin looked worried. "This will only take about an hour."

"Don't worry. She'll be back. And all alone." Nan drawled out *alooone*, clearly recovered from any offense over Reuben and back to matchmaking.

"Come on, Nan." Cassie headed for the door, then called to Martin. "I can't wait to see what you've done. I'll be back."

Cassie hadn't had more than a few minutes alone with Martin since well before all the rain. And after an hour of event planning with Nan, she was more than ready for a quiet moment with him. They'd seen Reuben drive down the lane in his wagon, which only garnered the slightest remark from Nan. Cassie suspected she was hiding some hurt from his insistence to stay away from her. She must know she was to blame for the rumors she'd indulged in repeating about the man. But it was none of Cassie's business, and her friend didn't seem inclined to talk about herself as much as she wanted to talk about Cassie and Martin.

There was nothing for Cassie to tell her. Truly over the past few weeks, she'd come to appreciate Martin as a friend more than ever. So much so, that she couldn't bear the idea of spoiling it. So she'd begged Nan not to interfere.

Nan hadn't exactly made any promises.

As her walk back to the bakehouse brought her up to Ada Beiler's cottage, she saw Martin waiting for her at the end of the bakehouse driveway. He waved and came to meet her.

Ada called to them from her front porch. "How's it coming along over there?" she asked, referring to the bakehouse. "I haven't seen you two for a few days. I reckon the rain slowed things down."

Martin took Cassie's hand when he reached her. Her heart sputtered at the gesture. But Martin held on to her hand and kept walking straight up to Ada's front steps, as natural as if they held hands every day.

Ada grinned just before Martin let her hand drop.

Cassie refused to blush no matter how hard her heart pounded.

Martin had taken her hand because it was easier than communicating with words. Words that would've gone something like, *Do you mind speaking with* Gammi *for a minute and then we'll be on our way*?

He hadn't pulled her along. If she'd resisted, he would have dropped her hand and spoken out loud. But she hadn't needed him to actually say the words. She'd learned how to interpret his nonverbal ones years ago.

He'd always chosen gestures over words when he could,

particularly before his speech improved in grade school. But even once he spoke well enough for everyone to understand him, he'd sometimes revert to signals in private. And the fact that he felt comfortable enough with her to still use his preferred means of communication was a compliment. Maybe more so than if he'd held her hand in a romantic sense.

Maybe. She didn't know because he never had.

She just wished her heart would settle down and accept his hand solely in the way he'd intended.

Martin did his best to be polite to his *gammi*. He forced himself to follow the rules of social convention and chit-chat with her. He hoped Cassie didn't mind. Of course, she probably wasn't as eager to return to the bakehouse as he was to finally reveal the project he'd worked on for weeks and been able to complete with the extra time in his *datt*'s workshop over the past few days.

He watched Cassie for clues to know when they'd chatted enough that it wouldn't be rude to leave. She conversed easily and knew how to draw him into the conversation when he struggled to listen.

Talking to his own grandmother wouldn't be hard if he wasn't so distracted. "*Gammi*, I'd like Cassie's opinion on something up at the bakehouse. Maybe we can visit some more later?"

There, that was polite enough, surely.

"Of course. Stop by anytime." His elderly grandmother leaned back into her rocking chair with a half grin on her face.

Goot. That meant he could go.

Cassie said her goodbyes and caught up with him before he crossed the road to walk up the driveway to the bakehouse.

He'd commissioned Reuben with making a sign to hang over the front gable, since signs were one of the man's specialties. But that was a surprise for another day.

Today, he'd reveal her new kitchen island, which he hoped exceeded her expectations.

He pulled a clean handkerchief from his pocket and paused before opening the screen door. Cassie noticed the cloth and paused in front of him.

"What's that for?"

"To blindfold you."

"*Vass?* Martin is that really necessary?"

"All *goot* surprises require a blindfold. Everyone knows this."

She threw her head back and laughed, then held out her hand. "Fine."

"Nay." He pulled the handkerchief out of her reach. "I have to do it, so you don't cheat."

One corner of her mouth tilted up in a half grin. "Okay, fine."

She gave a dramatic sigh but kept smiling, as he walked behind her to cover her eyes. He waved a hand in front of her face.

"I can feel the air from your hand, Martin. But don't worry. I can't see anything."

Guiding her by the shoulders, he took her through to the kitchen and stopped her in front of the new island before taking off the blindfold.

"Ta-da!" He sounded as giddy and childlike as he felt. He couldn't help it. He'd been looking forward to this moment and had worked through most of the night.

She didn't say anything, at first. Or even after several seconds. This was not the reaction he expected at all, and he began to worry.

Rushing around her, he pointed to the center of the structure. "It's a convection-style oven. The kind you said you'd like the most. And the electrician will be by tomorrow to hook it up."

He waited for a response. Nothing. "I know it's rather large, but that allowed for more cabinets and extra work space on the top." Still, nothing.

He turned slowly to face her, now afraid of the emotion he might see on her face. "We installed it facing the salesroom, but if you don't like it this way, I'll change…"

He was silenced by her sudden embrace as her arms wrapped around him. Momentarily startled, he didn't know what to think. But her nearness was pleasant, and before examining anything further, his own arms pulled her closer in a hug. She leaned back and he let her go, reluctantly.

"*Denki*, Martin." Her voice cracked, and he hoped with all his might he hadn't made her cry.

"Does that mean you like it?"

"Like it? Martin, it is absolutely beautiful. And maybe the most thoughtful thing anyone has ever done for me." She walked around the full perimeter, dragging her fingertips along the granite top. Then she opened the cabinets one by one. "You've even added pullout shelves."

"To make it easier for you to remove and put away heavy items."

"I… I can't possibly pay you what it's worth."

Now he was flabbergasted. "Pay me! Cass, it's a gift."

Her brown eyes widened and her lashes fluttered. He barely heard her whisper. "A gift?"

"*Ya*. I believe that is what they call it when someone gives something to another person without expecting payment."

"But Martin, what will people say? You can't just give me something this…this expensive and magnificent."

She definitely liked it. His heart stuttered between relief and the thrill of knowing he'd pleased her. "Then, don't tell anyone. I don't want any credit. I did it for you."

Her hand fluttered over her heart. "Truly?"

"Ya."

She pulled the handkerchief out of his hand and dabbed her eyes. "Don't worry. I'm not crying because I'm upset. I'm really happy."

He'd like another hug just to be sure, but didn't say so. "Then, I'm happy, too."

And he was. He didn't know any other way to tell her how important her friendship was to him. And even though holding her hand and receiving her hug made keeping his heart in the friend zone a little more difficult, those things also proved how special she was to him.

A friend who understood him without words was a priceless gift to him, more than he could ever repay with a bit of polished wood, granite and steel. And at least when he had to leave, she'd have this reminder that he cared for her.

Only, more and more, that didn't seem like enough.

Out of his peripheral vision he noticed a horse pulling a wagon trotting up to the side of the barn, visible through the kitchen window. Zach must have come to pick up Cassie.

"Zach's a little earlier than usual," he mentioned to her as he tilted his head toward the back door. "I'll probably stay here again, now that the place is aired out well. *Denki*, for that."

"I didn't know Zach was coming." She shrugged. "I left my bicycle down at the store to ride home." She held out his handkerchief, then pulled her hand back. *"Ach*, maybe I should wash it for you."

"That's not necessary. A few of your tears won't hurt me."

Her hand stilled in his as he reached for the cloth. Why didn't she let go of it?

"Cassie?" A deep voice came from behind Martin. "*Vass ist dass?* Have you been crying? Your eyes are red."

Martin's stomach twisted into a knot as he turned around to face the wrath of Eli Weaver. His face was redder than Cassie's eyes. In fact, Martin didn't think Cassie's eyes had been all that red. They'd been chocolate brown and warmed him with their sweetness only a few minutes ago.

"I haven't been crying, *Datt…*" She glanced at the island and appeared to think over her word choice before continuing. "The bakehouse is coming together better than I ever imagined it."

Eli tugged at his beard. His gaze bounced from Cassie to Martin and back again. Then he took a longer look at the island behind them.

Martin sensed Cassie stiffen, probably wondering what her *datt* would think if he knew Martin made it for her as a gift.

"*Ist dass* your handiwork?" Eli pinned Martin with his icy blue stare.

"*Ya*, though I can't take all the credit. My *datt* helped, of course." Only with the design details to ensure it all worked as intended, but Martin preferred Eli not know how much of the labor came straight from his heart.

"It looks *vell*-made." He nodded and turned to his daughter. "Time to go. Your *mamm* needs your help."

Cassie's mouth dropped open, and she covered it with her hand. "I forgot. *Ich bin* sorry." She turned to Martin. "I promised to help her make cookie dough to freeze for the Ascension Day festivities in a couple weeks."

She waited beside Martin as Eli left the room, then tucked his handkerchief into the palm of his hand.

"*Denki*, Martin. Your gift is too *wunnerbar* for words." And with that whispered affirmation, she followed after her father, leaving Martin transfixed and wholly unsure what had just happened.

Her hug had been sincere and lovely and perfectly chaste. Yet, his heart couldn't let it go, as if there was a message within he ought to comprehend. If only he had the courage to unravel and face it.

Chapter Eight

Two weeks later, Martin watched his sister's two children run across the yard from the Weaver's house to the Beiler's, where he sat on the front porch talking with his *datt*. "It's sure convenient for them to have two sets of grandparents living side by side."

Ezekiel Beiler nodded. Clearly the fact that Josh and Bethany were his *dochter*'s step*kinner* made no difference in how much his *datt* loved them. As soon as their feet hit the wooden steps, he stood to greet them with a pat on Josh's head and a squeeze around the shoulders for Bethany, who was nearly grown to his height.

"*Gammi* Leah has a plateful of cookies ready for you to carry back to your *Grossmammi* Weaver. But I also know she has two ice-cold glasses of *melka* and a couple extra cookies that wouldn't fit on the plate." Ezekiel winked at them both.

"And they're both for me!" Young Josh spun away from his sister to run inside.

"Oh, no, they are not!" Bethany lunged after him, and her brother's peals of laughter sounded through the screen door that slammed shut behind them.

"It's a mighty blessing your sister has so much family nearby to help when the *boppli* comes. Those two are a handful." The warmth in his father's tone indicated those two handfuls also claimed his *datt*'s full approval. "Your *mamm* sure can't wait for that *boppli* to arrive, though."

Martin leaned against the wooden slats of the rocking chair but kept the seat still. The view from his family's home stretched out wide over the sloping fields that ran like ribbons parallel to the mountain ridge silhouetted against the horizon. The scene wasn't much unlike the one from his own cabin.

The differences, though, came in other forms. There were no laughing children at his cabin, for one. He appreciated the silence there. And yet, the voices carrying out to them from inside the house came as an unexpectedly pleasant change.

His *datt* pressed his hands against the arms of his chair and rose to stand. *"Kumm mit mich."*

The simple request to follow him came with no explanation. Nor did Martin require one. Evening chores must be done. And Martin would help, whether asked or not. He and his *datt* fell into an easy rhythm. Some things didn't change, and this was a routine written into his DNA for generations.

The hay stores were getting low, he noticed as he pitched his fork deep into a mound to gather some feed for the horses overnight. His *datt* didn't like baled hay, and still gathered it the old-fashioned way.

"I reckon you'll be getting up hay soon. Since I won't be going anywhere for a while, I can help." Maybe Martin would save his family a little money, since his *datt* wouldn't have to hire as much help.

"You're meant to be keeping a watch over Cassie Weaver, ain't so?"

"Once I finish the renovations for her to open the store, I'm going to have time on my hands. I doubt she wants me hovering over her every day. I'm not sure what I'm meant to do until I…go back." He'd almost said leave, but the word choked him.

He didn't want to leave Cassie again.

"There's never a shortage of work to be done." His father pinned him with a gaze Martin could only feel as affectionate. "You're always welcome here, *sohn*. You know that, *ya*?"

"By you…and *Mamm*…*ya*, I know so."

Ezekiel stabbed his pitchfork into the hay and left it there.

"Leave it." He nodded at the tool in Martin's hand, then strode out toward the back field.

Dropping his pitchfork, Martin followed through the fields, then along the creek that marked the southernmost property line. The area was wooded, and they headed upstream toward the hunting cabin at the spring that fed the creek. But they weren't going that far, only to a rocky outcropping that hovered above his *datt*'s favorite fishing hole.

And they weren't stopping to fish. When *Datt* left the poles behind, it meant one thing. He was coming to talk—and to listen. This was the spot where Ezekiel Beiler brought Martin as a young *kinner* when he struggled to communicate. He gave Martin space to think and to talk, as slowly as he needed. And for as long as was necessary without distractions and constant interruptions.

If he ever brought Seth here for anything other than fishing, Martin wasn't aware of it. His brother never much liked fishing. *Nay*, their *datt* took Seth hunting, which Martin abhorred. This visiting spot was reserved for Martin. And apparently, his *datt* felt they needed a *goot* talk now because he squatted down to the ground, making a seat from the rock and leaning against the trunk of a tall pine.

Martin joined him, allowing the ripple of the water and the rustle of the leaves from above to soothe his mind and reset his heart rate to a tranquil pace. His senses filled with the aromas of pine sap and rich soil blended with the cool water, not long passed through the purifying rock from deep underground.

He loved this place.

And he loved his *datt* for making it so for him.

"I can't come back to stay, *Datt.*"

Ezekiel didn't argue or ask for a reason, just waited.

"I have a living down in the valley, and I've invested a lot in making beekeeping work. I couldn't have stayed much longer than three months, even if…" Martin let his concerns about Eli Weaver's feelings go unsaid. "Anyway, by early August I need to get back to my hives. *Onkel* Titus is going to check on them for me this month, but I'll have to begin collecting the summer's honey to sell."

His *datt* flipped a small twig back and forth between his fingers, thinking for a few beats before responding. "I remember when you wouldn't have been able to string that many words together. Not so quick. Not so as anyone other than your brother could interpret."

True. When Martin was little, before a special teacher came to their school and helped him learn to talk, his twin had been the only person who could decipher what Martin meant to say in his nonverbal way. But when Seth needed him, Martin had failed. "I'm sorry about Seth."

"He chose his way." His *datt* made no hesitation with his answer this time. "You are not to blame." The surety with which he spoke brought some comfort to Martin.

"*Denki* for saying so. But… I feel like I could have done more."

"*Ya*, we all do." His father cupped a hand over Martin's shoulder with a pat of reassurance. "But that is not why I brought you out here."

His *datt* rubbed at his knees momentarily before continuing. "You've made me proud, *sohn*. Not by the kind of pride that is a sin, but in the way a father feels for a *sohn* who has done well. Our Father in Heaven was well pleased with His Son. And so I am with you."

Martin's heart swelled. Such an admission was rare for an Amish father.

But his *datt* wasn't finished.

"You can do whatever you put your mind to do, Martin. With *Gott*'s help, you have done more than many a man has done with less to overcome."

"I cannot change Eli Weaver's mind." And that was the real reason Martin knew a future with Cassie was hopeless.

"You don't need to change Eli's mind about anything. You must only be the man *Gott* means for you to be. And if you love the minister's *dochter*, then you will love her well. No father could ask for more."

"I don't know, *Datt*." Was that the kind of love he felt for Cassie? He loved her, of course. But did he love her enough? How was he supposed to know?

"You will know when the time is right." His father raised to stand. "Perhaps you have been gone from this spot too long. Come here to clear your mind more often, and I think you'll figure it out."

Would he? If he hadn't figured it out over the past three years, could he really do so before time to leave again?

The last of the *kinner* were put to bed at their grandparents' house, and exhaustion draped over Cassie like a heavy quilt. It had been a long day, but the cool air of a mid-May evening beckoned before she stole away to bed herself. She quietly shut the door behind her as she stepped out onto the front porch. Recently vacated, the swing in the corner still moved, though slightly, emphasizing that she was alone. Descending the front step and looking up, she gazed into the moonlit night sky, where several stars blinked back at her from high above.

She chose the lower step for a seat and took in the unobstructed view. A shadowy figure emerged from the woods behind the Beilers' house. Though too far off to make out who it might be, she wasn't alarmed. The nearer he walked, the more confident she became it was Martin ambling toward the Beiler home.

She headed in that direction, slowly, in case she'd misjudged. How awkward it would be to meet another man in the night for no purpose. The thought froze her steps.

Ach, how silly she was being. When she laughed out loud at herself, the figure turned, having heard her she supposed, and approached with longer strides.

"Cass?" he called, leaving no question it was Martin. He came the rest of the way to her.

"I thought it was you." She fell into step beside him, giddy with delight at seeing him so unexpectedly. "Would you like to sit a spell?"

In the dimness of the evening, his face was shadowed, yet she detected a smile as he looked down at her. "*Ya*. I'd like that."

In no hurry, they returned to the front porch of her grandparents' home. And she felt a special pleasure knowing he wanted to linger there with her for a while.

"I've missed you." The words slipped out. "I mean, having your friendship at times like this…just to be together."

The more she tried to explain, the hotter her cheeks grew. She pressed her mouth closed before she made it worse.

"Me, too," he said simply before sitting on the top step and patting the spot beside him.

About to sit, she wondered if some refreshments might keep him longer. "Would you like a drink and maybe a cookie?"

His wide grin at that was unmistakable. "*Ya,* I've been in the woods a long time…thinking."

About what, she wondered. But didn't ask.

She slipped inside to get them both a tall glass of sweet tea and a small plate of goodies made for the holiday celebrations. Remembering the cookies Leah Beiler had sent, she added one to the plate for Martin.

He looked up at her when she handed him his drink and saw the plate of treats. "Is that one for me?"

"Unless you want to share it. I know how much you love your *mamm*'s whoopie pies." She'd eaten one earlier, but gave him a longing look as though she truly wanted some.

He eyed the plate as if in some great dilemma.

"Martin…" She sat the plate down between them and picked up the whoopie pie. "Here. I was only kidding."

He shook his head.

"You don't want it?"

"*Vass?*" His eyes met her questioning gaze, then glanced down at the chocolate cream cookie in her outstretched hand. "*Denki.*"

He took the cookie and dunked it…in his tea.

"Martin! Are you alright?"

"*Vass?*" He was becoming a broken record.

"You dipped your whoopie pie in your iced tea."

He looked at the dripping concoction he held in front

of his mouth. His eyes widened before looking for a place to put it down. She handed him a napkin, into which he wrapped the ruined treat, then placed it on the far side of them.

Cassie might've laughed if he hadn't appeared so deathly serious. And the silence that stretched between them began to worry her. Still, she didn't prod. It was best to give Martin time.

"Do you know why I left Promise?" He finally spoke and couldn't have surprised her more.

"Because Seth told you to." She clamped her lips shut.

He'd shocked the truth right out of her. They'd never talked about the subject outright. And her quick response was an opinion she'd buried somewhere deep inside for so long, she'd forgotten it. Seth was a painful subject. She probably shouldn't have brought him up. "*Ich bin* sorry."

His arm came around to rest across her shoulders. "You may always speak the truth with me, Cass. You don't need to apologize."

In an attempt to settle the butterflies in her stomach, she tried to imagine his hand over her shoulder as a brotherly touch. It didn't work. Imagining Martin as her brother was impossible.

Martin blew out a long breath and slowly dropped his arm back into his lap. She wished he hadn't, but the flight of the butterflies seemed to still. Honesty was good and all, but she wasn't about to confess this strange sensation to him.

"I've been out in the woods thinking about that. There were other reasons. Some don't matter anymore."

"But some do?"

"One."

Just one. Well, that couldn't be too difficult to fix, surely.

"What I want—really want—hasn't changed at all." His gaze was so intense she could barely hold it. "Three years later, though, and it still feels as impossible as ever."

"Can I help?" Her offer came out somewhat squeaky under his intense gaze, now filled with an emotion she hadn't seen before. Her mouth went dry, and she swallowed to try to explain. "I don't want you to leave again, Martin. If I can help you get what you want…will you stay?"

He gulped down his tea, chocolate crumbs and all, set down his glass and stood. "I can't answer that, Cass. Not honestly. Not yet."

She rose to stand in front of him, searching for a clue that would help her know what to say—what to do.

"Have you wondered why folks assume we are courting?" He stood so close, searching her face for clues to her emotions. "And what it might be like if we were?"

Her heart skipped a beat. He was full of unexpected questions tonight, and she held her tongue to keep another unbidden truth from escaping before she revealed how much and how long she'd dreamed of such a thing.

"*Mach's goot*, Cass." He was telling her goodbye even though their conversation felt very unfinished. Had she taken too long to answer? For sure, she hadn't meant to give him the impression that a courtship wasn't a favorable idea to her. Had she?

She couldn't let him think so.

"*Sayn dich meiya?*" she called after him, hoping he heard the invitation she offered.

"*Ya*, I'll see you tomorrow. You can count on that, Cass." His voice was strong and sure as he disappeared into the night.

Martin promised to see her tomorrow—a day with no work as an excuse to be together, but a perfect day for a couple courting in secret to see each other. Was she ridiculous to hope Martin thought the same? There'd be precious little rest for her tonight, as she couldn't wait to find out.

Chapter Nine

"Let's hope the whole day isn't ruined by rain. Those clouds look like a storm is building out there." Fern gazed through the window in Cassie's *grossmammi*'s kitchen before dipping her hands back into the soapy water to wash another breakfast plate. "I was thinking about Ascension Day last year. It's hard to believe how much has happened in our lives in just one year." Fern held a hand over her belly, and Cassie assumed she was referring to her soon-to-be-born *boppli*.

Cassie agreed with Fern. Much had happened. It was on this day a year ago that Martin had first shown his face back in Promise. Cassie recalled that particular morning as she, Fern and *Gammi* Weaver had done the dishes after the *kinner*'s sleepover. Though it had been a brilliantly sunny day, Cassie had been glum that day. She'd decided she must accept that Martin would never come back.

After chasing her cousins all that day, she'd gone to the apple orchard to rest in the shade. Seemingly, out of the blue, Martin found her there. Without a word, he'd leaned back against the tree where she sat and passed her a jar of honey.

"For your buns," he'd said.

She'd been so hopeful at the sight of him, but he hadn't stayed long.

Cassie sighed.

Water splashed across the countertop all the way from the sink to where Cassie was drying the dishes, jolting her back to the present. She pivoted toward Fern, who doubled over and groaned.

"*Ach*, Fern! To bed with you right now." *Gammi* Weaver rushed from the other side of the room. "These pains have been coming on you faster and faster all morning. Don't think I haven't noticed."

Cassie had noticed that Fern seemed uncomfortable, but she'd been so for weeks. The baby was overdue, and Fern had so many false starts to labor that she blew off any concerns at this point.

Judging by the seriousness on *Gammi* Weaver's face, this time was different.

Fern's lips pursed as she exhaled a long, slow breath. Her eyes were closed. Her nod barely noticeable. She wasn't going to disagree this time.

"Go find Nick," her *grossmammi* instructed Cassie. "He's likely in the barn with your *datt* preparing the hay wagon for the *kinner*'s ride."

"And my *mamm*, *bitte*." Fern's request came weakly as she leaned against her mother-in-law, who guided her toward the bedrooms.

Barefooted, wearing a wet apron and still clinging to a dish towel, Cassie ran outside. She'd been told to seek out Nick first, but somehow she felt Fern's *mamm* was needed the most urgently. So when she didn't see her *datt* or uncle at first glance in the barn, she raced toward the Beiler's house to find Leah.

Before reaching the house, she spotted Fern and Martin's *mamm*, whose white-streaked ginger hair was pulled under her head covering. She was kneeling down in her vegetable garden snipping lettuce. Cassie gasped for a breath before calling to her.

"Leah. *Kumm*. It's Fern." Cassie watched Leah as the message registered. Her head lifted away from her focus upon her task, and she dropped her basket full of greens.

Cassie doubted whether Leah could run. Her knees often gave her issues, and her cane wasn't anywhere in sight. Cassie held out her hand to offer support.

"Denki." She accepted Cassie's hand before pulling up to stand, then placed her other over her heart.

"I didn't mean to frighten you. It's just that when *Gammi* Weaver gives a command, you follow with all haste. And Fern asked for you."

Leah chuckled. *"Ya*, your *gammi* speaks with authority, for sure. And when it comes time for a *boppli*'s arrival, she knows what she is about."

Leah might not be able to run, but she surefire could walk faster than Cassie would've figured. As they neared the barn, she felt confident Fern's *mamm* would make it without her just fine. "I need to tell Nick."

"Go on. My knees seem to be carrying me better than usual." She released Cassie's arm. "Maybe after you find Nick, you can let Ezekiel and Martin know to be praying. They went fishing but ought to be on their way back by now. Their breakfast is keeping warm in the oven." Leah bit at her lower lip. "I don't want to frighten anyone, either. But I think it best if someone called help to be ready in case…"

By help, she must mean an *Englisch* driver. The nearest hospital was a thirty-minute drive. And they didn't deliver babies. The ride to the city hospital with an obstetrics unit could take over an hour.

"Twins can be tricky," Leah went on. "You'll make sure

Martin understands, won't you? He will know what to do. He knows."

What would Martin know? And twins—Leah Beiler nearly died delivering Martin and Seth, even Cassie had heard that tale. "Twins? But I thought twins came early."

Leah's brow pinched with worry. "If Martin and Ezekiel aren't back by the time you've told Nick, go to the store and call for help. You will do that, won't you? Don't let anyone talk you out of it."

"*Ya*, Leah. I will hurry." Why in the world had Fern and Nick been so hush-mouthed about the seriousness of this pregnancy? No wonder *Gammi* Weaver had been so forceful.

With more urgency than before, Cassie ran to her *dawdi*'s barn to find her uncle. With every pounding foot-fall, she prayed fervently that Martin would return from fishing soon.

Martin would know what to do. He had more knowl-edge of the outside world, and this was too important for Cassie to mess up.

Martin and his father each carried a pole and a line with freshly caught rainbow trout from their early trip to the fishing hole. He'd been reminded of how much fun the time spent with family and friends each Ascension Day had been growing up.

They emerged from the woods starving and eager for the delicious addition of grilled trout to their breakfast.

"Your *mamm* is going to love this," his *datt* repeated for at least the fourteenth time, and Martin had no responses left.

Out from the protection of the trees, the light drizzle they'd felt in the woods turned to a more drenching rain.

The sky had threatened to open all morning and now unleashed in earnest.

He tugged his hat tighter over his forehead to shield his sight and noticed a woman riding down the road on a bicycle.

"Bad timing for a bike ride. What do you suppose Cassie is up to?" his *datt* asked.

Martin squinted. Sure enough, Cassie was pedaling her heart out down the road.

"Cass," he called and waved.

She skidded to a stop. Mud splattered and the back tire slid out from under her. She righted the bike and pedaled hard toward them.

She was explaining that Fern was in labor before she came to a stop. As she dropped her bike and moved to stand in front of them, his *datt* took Martin's fishing pole and then the line of fish from his hands.

"Go quick," he said to Martin. "Take Sugar. It'll be the fastest way."

"I'm coming, too." Cassie propped a hand on her hip. "I told Leah I would. She made me promise not to be deterred. By anyone."

"Attagirl," his *datt* encouraged her, though why Martin couldn't fathom. She was already nearly soaked. And though they'd ridden together many times as children, they weren't so small anymore. He wasn't sure Sugar could handle them both.

"It'll take time to saddle another horse. Sugar is the only one who'll tolerate being ridden bareback."

"I'll go ahead on my bike." She reached for the mud-caked and thoroughly ancient thing at her feet.

"It has a flat tire, Cass." He pointed at the back tire that must have blown out earlier.

"Don't waste time arguing, you two," his *datt* cut in. "Sugar can handle you both, if that's what's worrying you. It's not far and you'll make *goot* time. Your *mamm* wouldn't ask this of you and Cassie without reason."

A victory smile lit up Cassie's expression, even as rivulets of water dripped down her face. His own shirt was plastered wet against his back. There wasn't time to reason further with either of them.

"Let's go then, before we drown."

Cassie dropped the bike and hurried after him to his *datt*'s barn where Sugar remained in her dry, comfortable stall.

"Hello, there, old friend." He approached the mare. "I have a mighty big favor to ask of you."

She whinnied a greeting back to him and allowed him to stroke her neck. Martin spoke as soothingly as he could, hoping not to spook her with their urgency. Sugar had an easygoing nature, but he doubted very much she'd appreciate hauling two grown folks on her back in the rain.

"I know you're comfortable and doubt you want to go out in the rain, but we need your help." He motioned for Cassie to come beside him. "Will you allow me to put her on your back?"

Sugar stilled in acquiescence, waiting for Cassie.

"Ready?" Martin asked Cassie this time. She nodded, and he lifted her toward the horse's haunches enough to leave room for him in front of her. "If I ride up front, you might not get as wet. I need you to carry me, too, okay?" he warned Sugar and readied to mount.

Cassie balanced herself and leaned back as far as she could as Martin swung into place, then she held tightly around his waist. He was cold and wet, but they were both soaked, so he supposed their nearness couldn't make it much worse for her. When they got to the store, she could go upstairs to Nick and Fern's living quarters and find dry clothing.

Oddly, he wasn't minding the discomfort of the situation near as much as he'd expect. Before he could think too long on the reason, he urged Sugar forward, and she kindly obliged despite the extra load and the dreary weather.

As the rain pelted him, he made a mental note of a much-needed addition for his growing list of things to be done before he left home again. He'd make sure to have a telephone shanty installed at his parents' house. A hassle like this for a phone call was ludicrous.

For sure, he wanted to spend time with Cassie today. But not like this.

The night before, when he'd walked out of the woods and saw her at her grandparents' house, he'd already been half-convinced to try and win Cassie's heart. Thinking on all his *datt* had said, especially the part about Eli, had been eye-opening. He'd been stuck, though, on the question of whether he could make Cassie happy simply by loving her. But as they'd talked on her grandparents' porch, he knew he had to find out.

Only, he hadn't a clue how a man went about a courtship at his age. He'd avoided all the courting traditions in his teenage years. He didn't have a buggy to steal her away for a midnight ride. And he wasn't assured to be welcome at a Sunday singing, if he did ask her to go out. Promise had no restaurants for a date. He was going to have to get creative.

And he was pretty positive that getting soaked while riding on the back of a smelly horse wasn't considered romantic by any woman. No matter how much he wanted to woo the minister's daughter, he had no idea where to begin.

Weaver's Amish Store came into view. He directed Sugar

toward the overhang on the side of the building where several hitching posts had been installed and she'd be protected from the worst of the rain.

Dismounting was going to be tricky, however, so he changed course to the front entrance where the porch was about the same height as the horse's belly. Cassie's foot dangled mere inches from the wooden edge. He twisted around and offered his arm. "Can you slip your arm through mine?" A memory flashed of hiding behind a barn with her and spying on a local square dance. "Like a do-si-do."

She crooked her elbow through his, and with an overwhelming jolt the full replay of the pair of them dancing in the grass with the fireflies zoomed through his mind.

He shook his head to hold the memory back. There wasn't time for reminiscing. Although realistic flashes like that were beyond his control, this one soon ended.

"Now," he instructed carefully, "hold the railing with your other hand and step onto the porch. I'll do my best to keep you balanced. Just don't pull me off with you."

"I'll try not to." Her lips turned up in a mischievous grin. "Can't make any promises."

He signaled her to go, while mostly confident Cassie wouldn't purposefully tug him off his mount. Her eyes followed the steps he'd laid out, then he felt the weight of her as she swung free of her seat. He held on to her until her footing was sure.

"Denki." Her face flushed, but she appeared fine otherwise, for which he was relieved.

"I'll meet you inside," he said before taking Sugar to tie her up. But when he returned, Cassie remained standing at the front door.

"It's locked." Her expression turned a little panicked.

"I don't have a key. I've never needed one before. And I didn't think."

He took the steps three at a time to reach her and get out of the rain. "They must keep a spare hidden somewhere."

"If so, I don't know where." Her shoulders sagged and her lower lip pouted. "How could I be such a *dummkopf* not to think of it before I left?"

"It will be alright, Cass. If we can't find the key, Nicely's gas station will be open today. *Englischers* don't close for much of any kind of holiday, much less an almost strictly Amish observance." He pointed to his sister's handwritten note taped to the door. "See, they have to be reminded of why the store is closed. How many customers do you suppose have already come here and read that sign today?"

"Your *mamm* was worried, Martin. I think we need to do whatever is fastest. Did you know Fern is having twins?"

He hadn't. And he didn't need an explanation for why that would be a concern. They could find the key and get dry when he returned. If Cassie waited here, she'd at least be out of the rain on the covered veranda, and he could run down Main Street faster than worrying with the horse again.

"Do you mind waiting here, while I go down to the station?" he asked.

She shook her head. "I don't believe we have any better option. I'll look around for the key while you're gone."

"Check the greenhouse around back. You'll be dry and warm in there, plus that's a sure place my sister might choose. I'll be back." He squeezed her hand goodbye, thankfully without any accompanying flashback.

"Go," Cassie ordered. "She said you'd know what to do."

He jogged down the steps and through the rain toward the gas station. He wasn't going to mess around. He'd call for an ambulance. The nearest volunteer fire and rescue would arrive faster than any driver he might attempt to get. Plus, the paramedics would know what to do and could get her to a hospital faster than any other means, if needed.

The truth was that he wasn't always his best in an emergency. But he'd trained himself to remain calm. There was always a solution near at hand, if he could zero in on how to solve the problem and shut down his natural inclination to panic. He'd gained a great deal of practice by working with bees.

But having his sister in danger was pushing him to the brink. She'd almost died once, when he was very young. If Nick Weaver hadn't happened to find her at the right time and pull her out of a house fire, she'd have suffered far worse than the scars she still bore.

His *mamm* had drilled the protocol for calling emergency services into both him and Seth after that. He had no second thoughts about what she expected him to do now. He channeled the growing adrenaline into his effort to reach Nicely's as fast as his legs would go against the pouring rain and the weighted rub of his waterlogged trousers.

Cassie finally found a key stashed behind a wall thermometer in the greenhouse, although she suspected it was a key to the entrance to their house rather than the store. The heat and humidity in the hothouse were more unbearable than the cool dampness outside, especially since the rain had eased. So she decided to return to the store and wait for Martin on the covered porch.

A chill breeze met her outside the greenhouse, making her teeth chatter. Martin was right. She'd need some dry clothes.

A siren wailed in the distance, and she recognized the

call of the volunteer fire department. The wail reached the store easily every time it went off. She suspected this time was Martin's doing. And soon local volunteers would rush down the road in their trucks to answer.

Relief flooded through her.

She was glad Martin had called the rescue squad instead of a driver. The Amish still preferred home births, and she had no doubt some folks would criticize his action as premature and unnecessary. Likely, Leah Beiler knew so, too. But Martin was the one she trusted to know what to do.

On her way around the building, Cassie paused to comfort Sugar, who snorted when a truck with flashing lights raced by. "You've been a *goot* girl. Did you know it was Fern you helped today?" Cassie was sure the horse would approve, if she did. Sugar was favored by all the Beilers, and she loved them back. "You know a treat is waiting for you, don't you."

If Cassie had an apple, she'd give her one now. She looked up to see Martin walking into the store's parking lot. He appeared exhausted and gave her a weary smile as he neared.

"Help is on the way. I'm sure it won't take them long." He propped an arm against the wall and rested his head against it. "Your *datt* won't be pleased with me. And you have to let me take all the blame, okay? You never said to call 911. You only meant for me to call a driver to be on standby."

"I'm glad you called the EMS. And if you'd have asked me first, I'd have totally agreed you should. My *gammi* and your *mamm* have never looked so serious to me in all my life."

He rubbed at his head. "It was the right thing to do. I'm not doubting that."

He'd only done as his mother had asked. Leah was also

Fern's mother. Her *datt* wouldn't be angry about such choices in an emergency. "*Datt* is not so unreasonable, Martin. He truly is not."

"Maybe I shouldn't have singled him out. But not everyone will agree with what I did. This is exactly the kind of thing that divides Amish folk."

"They'll settle their differences on this. They always do. One way or another, they find a common ground and move on. Besides, who wouldn't understand the need for caution in Fern's situation?"

"I don't know." The strained lines across Martin's forehead deepened. "But I'm an outsider now. This won't do me any favors if I want to change that fact."

He was concerned about the approval of the local Amish community. This was the first glimmer of hope he'd given that he may change his mind about staying in Promise.

"Do you not wish to be an outsider any longer, Martin?" Her heart pumped a little faster.

His green eyes pierced through the breath she'd been holding, causing her to sigh. He didn't have words. And the ones she conjured from his expression were too *wunnerbar* to believe.

He pushed off the wall and broke the spell. "Did you find the key?"

"I think I found the house key." The metal object was wrapped tightly in her fist.

"*Goot*. You're soaked and going to get sick. Why don't you go find something of my sister's to change into before we leave?"

"You seem a little bossy all of a sudden." The brisk change in his demeanor made her bristle.

"I'm tired and worried. Fern is having two *bopplis*. You are soaked, and the storm blew in a cold front." He took a deep breath and rubbed at his neck, but then lifted a brow as the corner of his lips tipped sideways. "I'd very much appreciate if you would change, so Eli doesn't also hold it against me when you show up looking like a ragamuffin and later perish of consumption."

She somehow kept a straight face, as much as she wanted to laugh at his dramatic explanation, which she knew was intended to mimic one of the novels she loved to read.

"A ragamuffin? What a compliment." She glared in mock outrage.

He sighed. "*Bitte*, Cass."

"I was teasing, Martin. I'm not that easily insulted." And if he hadn't made her worry that this incident would keep him from staying in Promise, she might actually be a touch flattered that he was worried over her. She examined his own rumpled state. "Speaking of which, you're not exactly at your best, either. I'm sure *Onkel* Nick has some dry pants up there, too."

"Lead the way, fair *maedel*." He grinned at her and motioned toward the house entrance.

Ach, Martin could be romantic, after all, if he ever decided to try.

She walked ahead before he could see her blush.

Then an image of her lock of hair in his pocket watch flashed through her thoughts. Again, she wondered, when had he taken it? What did it mean? And more so, would she ever know?

Chapter Ten

To avoid dripping water all over his sister's house, Martin remained in the sunroom to wait for Cassie. Trying on Nick's clothing wasn't necessary to know it wouldn't fit him. His brother-in-law was taller than him by at least four inches. Instead, he waited for Cassie to dress in something dry from his sister's closet. Then they could make a quick detour to the bakehouse where he had his own clothing.

He glanced around the room, which served as an entrance to Nick and Fern's house above the store. He'd come home last year for the big day, when Amish from several communities gathered to build the living quarters for his sister's family. Never would he have guessed then that he'd be considering returning to stay.

Cassie emerged from the upstairs portion of the house. He loved the way her dark hair curled in the humidity, but she'd tamed it back into place under her *kapp*. She pinched the fabric on each side of the plain lilac-colored dress to lift the hem and looked down at the skirt.

"Your sister is a fair amount taller than me, too, but hopefully I can manage not to trip." Cassie laughed. "At least I found a pair of leggings to wear underneath. Riding Sugar won't be so uncomfortable, not to mention it will be a sight more modest."

Martin coughed. He hadn't expected to hear so much about women's clothing or be forced to think about how different Cassie's appearance was from his sister's. He quite preferred Cassie's size. She wasn't as tall and lithe as his sister, but she was womanly, and her shape was much more attractive in his opinion.

He shook his head to clear it before his thoughts traveled to where they had no business. And since he couldn't manage to form a sentence at that moment, he opened the door for her.

"Is it that bad?" she asked as she passed him to step outside.

"Nay." He cleared his throat. "You look nice."

She appeared satisfied by the slight upturn of her mouth, and he prayed silently that was enough to end the discussion.

Lights flashed, and a siren blared as the local ambulance roared down Main Street. Martin's heart pounded. They needed to hurry back. As quickly as he could, Martin untied Sugar and walked her around to the front porch, where mounting would be easier. As soon as they were both seated, he headed down the main road in the same direction the paramedics had taken.

"Aren't you going to go by the farm first and change?" Cassie had leaned closer to him, and he could feel her chin on his shoulder.

He turned his head to the side so she could hear him. "I think maybe we better just get back."

"Ya," she responded as the siren's volume decreased. "It seems so."

Her grip around his middle tightened and her head pressed against his back. He suspected she was praying. He prayed silently, too, as the horse obediently carried them homeward.

He prayed for his sister and for the *bopplis* she was about to bear. He prayed for his *mamm* and Rhoda Weaver as they guided the birth, as well as for wisdom for the paramedics to know if intervention was necessary. And after he'd prayed for everyone and everything he could think to mention, he added a more selfish request for himself.

If *Gott* was willing, he prayed, let Eli understand Martin's motives toward Cassie were pure. He had no desire to hurt her. Not ever. And he still wasn't convinced he was worthy of her. But he couldn't deny how important she was to him or how much he wished staying here with her was an actual possibility.

Did he really need to go so soon to collect his honey? From experience, he figured he could push things forward another month, so far as the bees and honey were concerned. And right now, another month in Promise with Cassie sounded *wunnerbar*. But he'd given Eli Weaver his word that he would leave at the end of three months. Three months that were already halfway past.

How could he have known those three months would be the fastest in his life? Or that he would come to regret believing they were an imposition? He'd been a fool not to realize this time in Promise was a gift. He wished he'd had the wisdom to have bargained for longer.

Only he hadn't. And now, he had to keep his word.

Around a bend, his parents' house came into sight in the distance. Within a few more yards, the Weavers' farm would also be visible. And so far, the ambulance hadn't sped back down the road with Fern. The thought brought some comfort.

He'd much rather have called for help for no reason than the alternative. And truly, he didn't care what anyone else thought, not in so much as his sister's safety was concerned.

Their opinions couldn't outweigh his reasons for doing as he had, but he knew their opinions could affect the outcome of whether he was welcomed back into the fold or not. He'd never understood why some folks had to find a fault in any decision that used help from the outside world.

Truthfully, Eli had never been that way. Eli was fairminded, and Cassie was right to defend her *datt*. But if folks did complain, it was Eli who'd be called upon to handle the headache Martin's actions caused.

Maybe that shouldn't worry him as much as it did, especially since Cassie also believed Martin had done the right thing. He really needed to forget about it before his tendency to obsess over minor details took over.

As they neared the two houses, he could see the menfolk gathered outside. His *datt*, Nick and Eli were huddled together under a large oak tree. Zach was chasing after his younger cousins in some form of the game of tag. The ambulance was parked in the driveway and turned off, and he supposed the womenfolk were all inside.

Sugar walked up the driveway until they reached a spot beside Eli's horse and buggy. The minister was headed their way. His long legs made quick work of the distance, and his face was somber.

"Let me help you," Eli offered to Cassie, who took his hand for balance before swinging her leg over Sugar's back. Martin ignored the slight kick in his side and leaned forward to give her more room, as she reached for her father's shoulders and jumped down.

Martin ground his teeth. He knew how many books she'd read about romantic horse rides with dashing heroes. This was certainly far from romantic. He hadn't even been able to assist her down.

Despite the sternness of Eli's brow, Cassie peered up at

Martin where he still sat on Sugar's back. "*Denki*, for everything."

He wasn't a storybook hero, yet somehow the tenderness in her eyes as she caught his gaze made him feel as though he could be. To her.

Unwilling to ruin the moment by checking Eli's expression, he remained attentive to Cassie alone. He pinched the rim of his hat and tipped his head to her. "I'll be over as soon as I see to the horse."

She smiled and silently mouthed, *Farewell, brave knight*.

At least, he chose to believe he'd read her lips correctly, as he pulled on the reins and trotted the horse toward his father's barn. Even after he'd dried and brushed Sugar, he still reveled in the sweetness of Cassie's expression. His pleasure continued all the way until he walked into his parents' house to find a dry set of clothing. Only then did he consider that in six short weeks, he'd have to truly tell Cassie farewell.

And for him, it wasn't going to be a sweet goodbye. Not even close.

Five short minutes after Cassie walked into her grandparents' living room, the cry of a *boppli* split the air. Tears sprang to her eyes at the precious sound. *Gammi* Weaver came rushing down the hall and stopped when she saw Cassie.

"*Ach*, you're back. Run. Go tell the men it's a girl." A huge grin spread across her *grossmammi*'s face, reassuring Cassie that all was well. "Fern is doing an amazing job. Another *boppli* is coming, so keep praying."

Cassie pivoted to head back outside and saw her own *mamm* coming from the kitchen. She could see a dining chair had been pushed back from the table and a Bible lay open at the same place. Cassie's *mamm* was what some folks called a prayer warrior and no doubt had been praying this whole time.

As Cassie reached to push the screen door open, her *mamm* gently placed her hand atop Cassie's arm. "Go tell them, and when you come back, we will pray together."

As soon as Cassie returned from sharing the news with her uncle and the others, she found her mother holding a Bible, waiting for Cassie to join her on the sofa.

As Cassie sat beside her, her *mamm* opened up the Bible to Psalm 118 and read it aloud. *O give thanks unto the Lord; for he is good,* the words began, and she knew why her *mamm* had chosen this passage. They had so very much for which to give thanks.

The psalm was rather long, and when her *mamm* came to a verse that mentioned bees, her *mamm* glanced at Cassie with a sparkle in her eye that made Cassie's stomach flip.

Her *mamm* knew Cassie's heart. Of course she did. She wasn't matchmaking or insinuating anything. She was hoping with Cassie that things would work out. And Cassie loved her for it.

As she finished the reading, her *mamm* reverently closed the pages, then placed her delicate fingers on Cassie's cheek. "The Lord will help us through anything, my sweet Cassie. Trust Him with your heart first. The rest will come."

As they bowed in silent prayer, Cassie first thanked *Gott* for blessing her with the most *wunnerbar* mother in all the world and for bringing Fern safely through her first delivery. Then, she asked, with all her heart, for a safe second delivery for both Fern and the *boppli*.

Less than ten minutes later, a second wail pierced her ears. Mercy, these little ones had some strong lungs. Praise *Gott*. What a *wunnerbar goot* blessing.

"Another girl." *Gammi* Weaver appeared again, tired yet overjoyed. "The paramedics will stay and give Fern some medicine to make sure she doesn't lose too much blood, but everything went as well as any of us could hope for."

Cassie wanted to sag right down to the floor; she was so overwhelmed with relief. Instead, she hurried back outside to deliver the message and tell Uncle Nick to come meet his newborn *dochters*.

Cassie's *datt* clapped his brother on the back with heartfelt congratulations. Then, Uncle Nick motioned for Ezekiel Beiler and *Dawdi* Dan to join him on his way to the house. Nick's voice was filled with emotion as he said to the two grandfathers, "*Kumm* with me and meet your *kinskinner.*"

When the two men left, Cassie remained under the oak tree with Martin and her *datt*. Martin had changed his clothing. His hair was still wet and slicked back, appearing a darker brown than usual. He bore his weight on his right leg, which tilted him ever so slightly away from her *datt*, who stood to his left.

She wondered if her *datt* knew how uneasy Martin was around him. He didn't seem to notice, and for sure didn't make an effort to alleviate Martin's discomfort. Still, she couldn't imagine her father disapproved of Martin the way he feared.

Her *datt* had never hesitated to show his dislike for any fella who took a special liking to Cassie. But Martin had never asked Cassie to go out riding or attend a singing, like those young men had done. Once at a cousin's wedding, her *datt* had wedged himself right between her and a boy who'd had enough courage to sit beside her at the marriage supper. She was long over the mortification. She hadn't much liked the boy herself. But still.

A throat cleared, and she looked up to see Martin pleading with his eyes for her help. Had they been talking? Without knowing what they'd said, she was at a loss to assist him.

"*Vass?* My thoughts were elsewhere." As embarrassing as the admission was, what else could she say?

"Martin offered to take you home. And I said that you've had a long day helping with the *kinner* and then an unexpected emergency. Would you like to go home to rest?" Her *datt*'s expression filled with concern.

"*Ya*, I am tired. I suppose I didn't realize how much until the relief of all being well was over." She hoped beyond hope he meant to allow Martin to take her home, although he could intend to do so himself.

"*Vell*, then, you may take my buggy," her *datt* said to Martin. "Of course, you will return soon enough. We won't need it in the meantime." A concession with a stipulation attached. Martin was not to remain alone with her overlong, but return quickly.

"*Denki*, Eli. I will be back shortly."

Inwardly, Cassie couldn't help but be a little thrilled that her *datt* conceded to allow Martin to drive her home. She counted it a victory, if only a small one. "*Denki, Datt.*"

As they walked to the buggy, Martin kept his thumbs hooked through his suspenders. He was still uptight about something.

"I am *wunnerbar* glad we won't be riding Sugar in the rain this time." She hoped to lighten his mood.

"It's not raining." His tone was terse. He didn't look her way, and he walked so quickly she had to double step to keep up.

"If you didn't want to take me home, Martin, I'm sure you didn't have to."

He didn't respond, or even send her a nonverbal cue—

other than his continued grimace. Her pleasure from her *datt*'s approval popped as surely as if Martin punctured it with a needle.

Why was he in such a cross mood? His sister was healthy and so were her two newborns. Cassie's *datt* was clearly not upset, as Martin had feared. She couldn't imagine how Martin was still worried that he'd be in trouble with her *datt* after he offered the use of his buggy to take her home. Perhaps Martin didn't realize how protective Cassie's *datt* had been all the years he was gone.

Still, grumpy as he seemed, Martin opened the buggy door for her. And Cassie couldn't help but notice that even at his worst, Martin was still more chivalrous than most Amish men she knew.

Did he and her *datt* discuss something she didn't know about? Was he embarrassed that he didn't have a buggy of his own?

She ought to just ask. But honestly, she was truly too exhausted to figure out Martin Beiler's mood this time. Suddenly, she wasn't in the mood to talk, either. Clearly, it didn't matter that her father expected Martin to return as soon as he'd dropped her off.

Tomorrow wasn't a holiday. They'd be back to work readying the bakehouse for the grand opening, which was two short weeks away. Staying busy had kept her sane these past six weeks with Martin. And if he was as determined as ever to leave Promise at the end of the next six weeks, then remaining busy was for the best. As, obviously, a day of no work had become nothing remotely resembling a day of secret courtship.

The drive to her parents' house would take them all the way back to Main Street and then in the opposite direction from the store. Rather than anything remotely romantic, it was going to be a long, uneasy ride.

Martin wasn't such a *dummkopf* that he didn't realize Cassie was offended and mad at him. He also knew he was all to blame, but it was going to take him a few minutes to get beyond the internal state he'd worked himself into.

Why did he have to be this way?

His parents would tell him because *Gott* made him to be exactly as he was for a purpose. Some days that required more faith to believe than others. Like now, when he'd held himself together through a crisis, but his body had reached its limit and his neurological system was overwhelmed to the point of shutting down. He shouldn't have offered to bring Cassie home. He should have gone somewhere quiet to rest.

To be alone.

In fact, he was currently terrified he'd explode and throw a tantrum the way he'd often done as a child. He was using all the control he could muster and knew he had precious little left.

And he was fairly confident that Cassie would rather be anywhere than with him right now. "*Ich bin* sorry, Cass. I just can't…can't anything right now."

He felt the tension between them lessen, but she remained still and silent beside him. His anxiety had radiated off of him to her. She didn't deserve this.

"*Ich bin* sorry," he repeated.

The warmth of her delicate hand wrapped around his bicep. "I forgive you."

She let her hand remain on his arm, infusing him with some renewed strength. Maybe at a better time, he'd have the ability to explain what was happening to him. He desperately wanted her to understand, though often he didn't understand himself. The triggers for these attacks weren't always so obvious.

"It has been a long day already, Martin, and a difficult one." Her voice was soft, as if she knew he was overwrought and needed quiet. "You must come into the house and eat. You didn't have time for breakfast, and then we never even had lunch. Some food will help, *ya*?"

He nodded.

How could he deny her? He wanted to be alone, but Cassie was the next best option. And he was hungry.

The rest of the drive to Cassie's passed in a peaceful silence, rather than the tense way it had begun. And slowly, slowly, he felt his nerves begin to untangle. Sending *Gott* an unspoken thanks for Cassie Weaver, he pulled into her driveway.

He couldn't stay long. He'd caught Eli's meaning plain enough.

The day hadn't gone anything like he'd dare to imagine possible. The night before when he'd sat under the stars with Cass, he'd started to believe that maybe he could win Cassie's heart. Could be good enough for her. But this day sure hadn't lived up to any of his expectations when he'd promised to see her today. And maybe it was for the best that those dreams settled back down into reality.

And yet, he promised himself this time, he'd make up this ruined day to Cassie somehow. Too bad he had such a limited time to figure out how.

Chapter Eleven

Cassie hadn't seen much of Martin over the past few days. Over the two weeks following Ascension Day, he and Zach had finished installing all of her shelving and completed the ramp at the entrance. The last she'd seen of Martin was three days earlier, when he'd hung a beautifully carved sign across the gable of the covered porch.

Martin had commissioned Reuben Bender to make the sign as a surprise for her, officially converting the farmhouse into Cassie's Country Bakehouse. She'd been fully occupied by being the baker since, while Martin had borrowed one of his father's packhorses and rode off to do whatever beekeeper-ish stuff beekeepers did.

Nan kept her company for several days and enjoyed setting up the salesroom. She was a bit of a whiz at organizing the place. So, while Cass feverishly baked ahead of the grand opening, her friend busied herself doing almost all the other work required to get everything ready for customers.

Tomorrow was the grand opening, and as much as Cassie missed Martin being around all the time, it may have been for the best. Because his presence had become more of a distraction than simply keeping busy could compensate for. She thought about him all the time and was certain she dreamed about him, too.

It wasn't healthy, especially since he was going to walk right back out of her life at the end of next month. She should get used to seeing him less now.

Or so she kept telling herself.

"Hey, Cassie," Nan called from the mudroom turned storage pantry. "I don't think handling this kind of delivery is in my job description."

Cassie tossed the sheet pan of cookies into the oven and set the timer before going to see what the fuss was about. "Since I'm not paying you, Nan, I don't think you *have* to do anything."

Cassie's teasing laugh came to a halt when she saw Nan's wide eyes as she stared at the package at her feet.

"*Nay.* I don't, but what I meant was I don't think this is in *your* job description." She looked up at Cassie. "I dropped it when I realized it's a shipment of queen bees for Martin. What are we going to do?"

"*We* aren't going to do anything. Leave it right there for Martin," Cassie decided with confidence. Neither she nor her friend knew the first thing about bees. Martin could have at least warned her or told her what to do.

"If you're sure." Nan backed away from the box. "You don't think they can get out, do you?"

Cassie looked around the small room for the smoker, but Martin must have moved it elsewhere since they'd rearranged this room. "If the bees could get out, let's hope they already did so on the way here."

She pulled Nan out of the room with her and shut the door, which nearly always remained open, then gave an extra tug to ensure it was fully closed. The latch clicked and both women breathed a sigh.

"Honestly." Nan shook her head. "You and Martin are

the most mismatched pair. Yet, you go together like bees and honey. You being the honey, of course."

"What do you mean? I might have a fear of bees, but Martin and I have plenty in common. Besides, he makes me..." Cassie clamped her mouth tight. She'd almost been tricked into confessing her growing feelings for Martin.

"*Ach*, Cassie. We've been friends for so long. I know I have a tendency to gossip, but I am trying to do better. And you can't think me so bad that I'd tell your secrets."

Not on purpose, she didn't. But it wasn't that. "It just doesn't feel right to say things that I haven't even told him."

Nan heaved a dramatic sigh. "In that way you and Martin Beiler do have one thing in common. You are both the most secretive folks about your feelings I have ever met. And yet, you both wear them right on your sleeves. It's so apparent, no one could doubt how either of you feels about the other. The only people left guessing are the two of you."

Cassie disagreed. Nan didn't know Martin the way she did. Her friend had no idea how complicated the man's feelings were. She only saw what she wanted to see, which was always a juicy story. But Cassie had no desire to argue after Nan had been so *wunnerbar* helpful.

The cookie timer dinged. Happy for the interruption, Cassie removed the baked trayful and slid another prepared tray into the oven, then reset the timer.

"Hopefully, he'll be back soon and can take care of those bees." Nan was peering out the window. "My *mamm* is excited about the hives he's setting up in Reuben's lavender fields. She says it will be amazing honey." Nan whirled around. "You really should sell it here. And I know the perfect area for a lovely honey display. I could even dry some flowers and make a pretty presentation for it." Nan's face glowed with excitement as it always did when she was creating a new idea. "Have you seen how many pretty colored boxes he has out there now?"

Cassie hadn't. She'd been busy at the bakehouse. "I don't go looking for bees or their hives, Nan."

"Well, you ought to at least see these from a distance." Nan pushed away from the window and began wrapping the cooled cookies in sets for the sale the next day. "Once this grand opening is done, you really should see how much work Martin has done."

Cassie felt a little guilty from the way Nan pushed. If she was Martin's friend, then she oughtn't be the last person in Promise to know what he'd been up to. "I suppose I've been so busy here that I didn't think about it."

"Oh, I'm sure Martin thinks nothing of it. But when you see, maybe you'll understand why everyone thinks he is planning to stay awhile."

"Stop. Don't start such a rumor because he is not. I know that for a fact." And getting Cassie's hopes up this way was almost cruel. "But you are right. I should go see because that's what *friends* do."

"And you'll see that I'm right, Cassie Weaver. Just you wait."

Cassie beat the cream filling for the whoopie pies with some extra vigor and let the subject drop. Nan had no idea how much Cassie would love to be wrong this time. But she refused to raise her expectations. Martin hadn't promised her anything beyond three months. Two of which were already gone. Her heart was already sure to be crushed without any extra help.

"What's next?" Nan wrapped the last of the prepared cookies. "Tomorrow's volunteers will be here bright and early, and they can help tie up any loose ends." Nan looked around, then raised both of her arms to shoulder height, bent at the elbows with palms out. "I'm not sure anything needs to be finished, though, other than the cookies you have in the oven."

"You've done so much, Nan, and probably know better than I do what has to be done before tomorrow. I really appreciate that you've helped so I can focus on baking."

"Your baked goods are what will make this a roaring success. Any Amish woman can cook, but you have a special touch. One stop at Cassie's Country Bakehouse is all it will take. Tourists or locals, your customers will look forward to the next time they can have more." Nan tapped the tops of the trays full of wrapped cookies for emphasis. "These will disappear tomorrow. I don't think you could make too many. You know how people flock to the Blue Ridge Parkway on Memorial Day weekend. I just hope the volunteers can keep up. And once the tourists slow down, plenty of folks around Promise are talking about how exciting it will be to have our own bakery. You really need to consider taking special orders."

"I plan to, Nan. I just need to get through the opening first."

"Imagine how much business you could bring in for the Fourth of July. Get ready. You're going to be hiring all sorts of help by that time."

"*Ach*, Nan, from your lips to *Gott*'s ears. I pray all is so blessed." Her friend was naturally exuberant and effusive. Yet, after being with steady, sensible, quiet Martin so much, Nan's nonstop praise was making Cassie uncomfortable. Still, she prayed all of this work paid off as well as Nan seemed to believe it would.

Once Nan left for the day, and Cassie had finished washing her mixing bowls and utensils, she began to wonder if she'd see Martin before Zach came to drive her home.

Right about when she'd decided to leave him a note about the package of queen bees safely trapped in the back storeroom, she heard the door open.

Martin stepped through the door while sliding his pocketknife through the packing tape of the dreaded box.

"Stop!" She jumped back as she shouted. "Don't open that in here."

Martin's head jerked up and his brow pinched together. "Why not?"

"Are you serious? Do you know what that is?" She took a cautious step backward.

"*Ya.* Do you?" He stepped farther into the room. Dangerously close, in her opinion.

She began a steady pace backward, aiming for the front exit to escape. "Stop following me."

"It's only a book, Cass." He pulled a thin paperback volume out of the box. "*A Beekeeper's Guide to Southeastern Mountain Flora.*" He held it up for her to see.

Mortification seemed to stop her blood flow. Had she ever been so embarrassed? She'd get Nan back for this.

Martin rubbed at his nose to hide a grin, but she still saw it before he turned the box upside down and gave it a shake. An air-filled plastic shipping bubble floated to the floor.

He came closer. Nothing but a box between them. He smelled of leather, lavender and creek water, and she wondered where he'd been all day. Quite a few places by the smell of him.

He held up the book. "What did you think it was?"

"Nan said it was a shipment of queen bees. That's why I left the package on the floor and shut the door to the kitchen." She motioned to the area as if it was still high risk. Her heart hadn't stopped pounding yet.

Martin twisted to look at the storeroom. He scratched

his head, then turned back to face Cassie. "I wouldn't have guessed Nan knew enough about bees to realize you can order queens through the mail. And I wouldn't have them shipped to your bakehouse, Cass." His green eyes settled into hers, searching deeply and making her heart flutter back to life. "I'm sorry you believed I would."

She forced a swallow in order to speak around the lump in her throat. "I should've known better."

"At least you won't have to worry about it again." He smiled and broke eye contact. "I left my books at the cabin. Mostly, I can do without them, but I've found a few flowering plants I need help to identify."

"I might be able to help." Traipsing through the mountain hills and vales with Martin might be fun, too. "My *mamm*'s always pointing out the wildflowers when we go mushroom hunting."

His eyes flashed back to her with interest. "After tomorrow, I can take you with me anytime you'd like to go."

"I'd like that." In fact, she'd happily join him anytime she could. "I think everything is about set for the big day tomorrow. You will stay for a little while, I hope. I know you've been busy with your bees. Nan says..." She stopped.

Cassie didn't really want to discuss Nan right now, or admit that she'd paid less attention to what Martin was doing than her friend had. Nan even knew about queen bees coming in the mail.

"I'll be around tomorrow." He placed the book into the box and set them on the counter beside the cash register. "Zach is coming early to help me set up the tables outside and post the signs Nan made. And I'll be available to do whatever you need the rest of the day."

"I don't expect you to do much. There will be so many people." She sure hoped there would be, anyway.

"I'll be alright, Cass." He winked. "I can always escape for some solitude, if it gets too overwhelming. I want to be here for you."

And she wanted to tip up on her toes and kiss his cheek. Martin could be sweeter than honey. But she didn't dare.

The way Cassie was looking at him, Martin would gladly spend all evening with her, right here, just the two of them. But he knew she needed to be home for supper. The Weavers ate promptly at 6:30 p.m., so they needed to get a move on.

He cleared his throat. "Anything left to do here? I can take care of it later, but it's already after six."

"I know. I'm ready to go, but where do you think Zach is?" An eyebrow quirked upward, and her hand went to her hip.

Martin cleared his throat to explain. "He asked me to bring you home. I thought he told you."

She cocked her head sideways. "Are we going to ride Sugar and the packhorse?"

"*Nay*, not this time." He'd been a little humiliated by not having a proper means to travel with her. The memory was a bit of a sore spot, but he'd rectified that issue for the time being. "*Kumm*, I'll show you."

He loved how her chin tipped up when she was curious, and wasn't at all surprised she beat him out the door. She stopped at the top of the steps and looked down at his new buggy.

"Martin Beiler!" She whirled around to where he stood behind her. "You didn't?"

He nodded.

She turned back to look at the somewhat aging courting buggy he'd bartered off of Reuben Bender for a share of his coming harvest. The thing could hardly be called new, except that it was for him.

"You did," she whispered.

"I could have borrowed my *datt*'s wagon for work, but the packhorse is working out well for what I need. Still, I thought this might come in handy for...when you need a ride." Martin had considered all the ways he thought Cassie might interpret this decision. The only one that worried him was the one he most suspected was coming.

"Does this mean you're going to stay in Promise?"

She had to jump straight to the question he couldn't answer yet.

"It means that while I am here, I can take you places." He could see her disappointment with his answer and tried not to take it personally. He'd hoped his prepared response would mean at least a little something to her. After all, he'd bought a courting buggy just to spend time with her. "Wouldn't you be willing to ride out with me sometimes, Cassie? You're working very hard. I thought you'd like a break on occasion."

"I just didn't think you'd buy a buggy when you're only here for another month. It doesn't make sense."

"Well, Cass, I did. And it is currently your ride home." He strode past her. What did it take to romance such a stubborn woman?

He turned to assist her up. "I'm also invited to supper, unless you think I shouldn't stay, since I have to leave again in four weeks."

She took his hand, but made no effort to climb into the buggy. "I didn't mean it that way. It's just very hard..." To find the words? He knew how that felt as he waited for her to finish. "It's hard to think about you leaving."

That was something in his favor, he supposed. He sure didn't want to think about leaving, either. He steadied her as she settled into her seat. Then, before releasing her hand, he squeezed her fingers and brushed a light kiss against the top of her hand.

When he eased his grasp, she held on to his hand a moment longer. Her brown eyes widened and her mouth dropped open. He waited, but she didn't say anything before finally closing her mouth silently and releasing his hand.

Cassie had never been speechless before. Maybe he had finally done something right. He'd spent plenty a night alone in his cabin. Enough to read a few of those books she loved and have some clue about her idea of romance, after all.

Admittedly, the gesture may have affected him more than it did Cassie. He couldn't tell, for sure. Moments like this would be his undoing if he wasn't able to win her heart in the end.

"Cass," he said as he straightened. "Let's make a deal. For the next month, let's live in the day and see what happens." And when he was forced to fulfill his promise to her father to leave, Martin could only hope she'd still wish for him to stay.

Chapter Twelve

The Friday morning of the grand opening of Cassie's Country Bakehouse dawned without a cloud in the sky. Promise was bound to be crawling with tourists traveling along the Blue Ridge Parkway all weekend. While Martin would normally choose a weekend like this to take a hike along some backwoods trails or explore new out-of-the-way locations his bees might love, today was all for Cassie.

And he was thrilled for her. A strong opening weekend of sales would be a real boost for her after all the hard work she'd done to make this day happen.

He'd had a dream the night before in which he was alone in his cabin. He could hear Cassie in the distance, and in the bizarre manner of a dream, he'd been aware of her new bakery opening. Only he'd had no part in it. And try as he might, he couldn't get to Promise to join her.

After waking, the angst of the dream remained several minutes. He couldn't help but wonder at how close the dream was to a reality that might have been, if he hadn't come back to Promise. He hadn't liked the feeling. And rather than go back to sleep, he'd hiked up to the meadow where he'd come two months ago to set up his first high mountain beeyard. There, lying under the tree where Cassie had attracted the attention of the swarm with her sweet cinnamon buns, he'd waited for the sunrise.

And now it was time to head back to the house to *redd up*. Zach and Cassie wouldn't be far behind the sun in their arrival. They had a lot to do.

Sure enough, by the time he came down from his upstairs washroom in fresh clothes, Cassie was in the kitchen hard at work. Her gentle humming met his ears before he saw her, and he stopped halfway down the stairs to listen.

"In the Sweet By and By," an old hymn, sounded as much like heaven to him coming from her lips as the other world that inspired the melody.

There's a land that is fairer than day,
And by faith we shall see it afar...

The words reminded him of his dream in which it seemed as though Cassie existed in a far-off land—one he couldn't quite reach. And he no more wanted to miss a day with Cassie here in this life than he would choose to miss Heaven in the next.

While he hated to ruin the moment, his feet drifted in her direction as if of their own accord. He waited to speak until she turned from her task and noticed him in the widened opening to the kitchen.

"*Goot mariye*, Cass."

"*Goot mariye.*" She smiled, then reached for an item wrapped in brown paper. "I brought you a breakfast sandwich." She held it out to him. "And the *kaffi* is almost ready."

"Mmm." Sausage and eggs between two slices of toasted homemade bread wasn't anything fancy, but it smelled *wunnerbar* to him—as did the coffee. "*Denki*, Cass. I am starving. I've been up since... I'm not sure exactly. Long before dawn, though. Sorry I didn't make the *kaffi*. I went outside and just came back a bit ago."

"No matter. Now it will be hot to go with your breakfast. Why don't you pull up a stool and I'll join you." She motioned to the far side of the kitchen island before pulling two mugs out of a cabinet and some fresh cream from the icebox. Then she grabbed the percolator off the stove. "Nan's bringing the giant urn we all share for weddings and such, but who can wait for that?"

"Not me," he agreed.

Her smile, along with the lightness of her tone, was infectious in its happiness. Martin found himself grinning as she filled his cup and added a heavy dose of cream on top.

"Just the way I like it, *denki*." He bowed his head for a short and silent thanksgiving for his unexpected breakfast. Then she settled onto the other stool he'd pulled around for her. "I believe this will be a *wunnerbar goot* day for you, Cass. Do you feel it?"

"I feel excited, *ya*, but also nervous. It's hard to believe this is really happening." She drew her *kaffi* mug to her lips and took several quick sips from the top where the hot liquid had cooled enough to swallow.

Martin sensed she was pondering a further response and so took a large bite of the scrambled egg and sausage sandwich she'd made for him. It was as delicious as supper had been the evening before. Cass and her *mamm* were both excellent cooks. Either of them might've made his tasty breakfast.

She looked over to him and smiled, as if she knew how much he liked that first bite, then took another sip of her drink before speaking. "Can I tell you something that might sound a little strange?"

He almost laughed. She could tell him anything she

wanted, of course. He took an even larger bite and raised an eyebrow at her, waiting for her to explain.

"I woke early this morning, too. I've been confused lately by my *datt*'s behavior. But I trust him. He's never been unkind, you know? I mean, he always only wants what is best for all of us—his *kinner*, of course, but also all of those *Gott* has placed in our little flock here in Promise. He has a shepherd's heart."

Eli Weaver loved his *dochter* with a fierce protectiveness, that was true. Yet, he could strike fear in the heart of any man interested in Cassie. And Martin thought he might understand that better than even Cassie could. She was worth protecting. No man but the best ought to have her.

"Anyway, the thought that occurred to me this morning was that I could trust *Gott* with this day, the same as I trust *Datt* in other things." With a sideways glance, she caught him staring at her. Her eyes welled up, just barely. Behind her emotion, it seemed to him, was a plea to understand that he was one of the *things*.

He knew she hoped he'd return to Promise to stay. She was Amish. They stuck together. But would she ever want him to stay for her? For more?

Martin nodded to her, encouraging her to continue.

"So, I prayed for *Gott*'s will to be done, and I meant it. I know we are always supposed to mean it, but this was different. I felt a comforting peace that no matter what happens with the bakehouse—with…with everything—*Gott*'s love won't fail me. He'll see me through."

She stared down at her fingers wrapped around the mug. "*Ach*, it doesn't sound as comforting out loud as it felt in my heart. Saying the words takes something away from it. As if what I felt was no more than the same old teachings we hear every church meeting." She looked up at him, her eyes glistening with restrained emotion. "But it was more, Martin, so very personal for me. Honest it was. I didn't imagine it."

He hadn't imagined his dream, either. The one in which Cass was happy— without him. Because *Gott* would fulfill her purpose one way or the other. And the choice was his to make, whether to be a part of her life.

Or not.

He knew without a doubt which option he most desperately wanted.

"I know what it is for words to fall short." He lay his fingers in the curve of her wrist where she still held her mug. "But I hear your heart, Cass, and believe with all of mine that *Gott* has only the best in store for you today."

"*Denki*, Martin." She made a hurried swipe at her eyes, and his hand fell away. "I'm so glad you understand."

He pushed back from the island counter and picked up the remainder of his sandwich to take with him. "I better go help Zach. Someone has to make sure he works at least part of the day. Once the girls start to show up, he'll be lost to us."

"Too true." Cassie rolled her eyes. "You better make the most of his help while you can. I have some last-minute chores to do before Nan and the volunteers show up, too." She grabbed her *kaffi* and paused. "That reminds me. Do you know when your *Onkel* Titus is coming? I'd hoped to put your honey out for sale. Nan even made a pretty dried flower arrangement and some paper bees to display on the table with them. And she already has plans for a display of your lavender honey after your summer harvest from Reuben's farm."

Martin thought Nan must have too much time on her hands if she was making paper bees, but Cassie's eyes sparkled as if Nan had done the most endearing favor. And he had to concede it was a selfless act of kindness on Nan's part.

For sure, Cassie had a close and caring community of support all around her. And not only from her best friend and family, *nay*, the entire community, both Amish and *Englisch*, were abuzz with excitement and support for her bakery.

She was sure to prosper, with or without Martin. He was glad for her happiness and security. But not at all happy to think of not being a part of her world.

And he'd prefer to be more involved than a few jars of honey bearing his name.

"Martin?"

What had she asked him? He tried to remember. Right, she wanted to know when *Onkel* Titus was coming. "He'll likely show up at some point later today after work. He was going to check on some of my beeyards for me, too, so he could arrive as late as tomorrow."

"*Wunnerbar.* At least we'll have honey on the shelves by Monday." She smiled prettily and gave him a little wave as he went off to find her *bruder*, Zach.

Martin found Zach, and the two made quick work setting up the tables outside for Cass. And as he worked, Martin remained thankful he was here for this day, at least, and prayed he'd be granted a way to spend a great many more special days with Cassie.

Martin wasn't wrong about her brother. As soon as Nan and the volunteers arrived, Zach made a beeline for the two single young women who'd come to help. Cassie had noticed his attempts to charm them from both near and far all morning.

Everyone knew Zach was a flirt, and he must enjoy living up to his reputation because he showed no indication of slowing. And woe to the girl who tried to ignore him. He'd just try harder.

Zach was in every way Martin's opposite, and exactly the kind of fellow her *datt* would shoo away from her. Of course, he did that to all the men.

Last night, he hadn't.

In fact, supper time with Martin and the game of Dutch Blitz they'd played together afterward as a family had been so ordinary and fun that Cassie hadn't noticed anything different. Martin had been so comfortable and accepted as a regular part of the family that she hadn't paused to think about how remarkable that was in the moment.

But she'd sure wondered on it as she'd fallen asleep last night. And she couldn't help but hope that Martin had noticed her *datt*'s acceptance, as well.

"I believe the signs we made are working." Nan leaned into Cassie's side and spoke low into her ear. "There's been a steady flow of traffic from Main Street to the bakehouse for the past hour or longer."

"You mean the signs that you made? I don't know how I'd have managed without you." They stood side by side behind a collapsible table covered with a white tablecloth and loaded with baked goods that were steadily disappearing. When any particular item was almost gone, an efficient volunteer showed up with an extra supply.

"You had your hands full making all of this." Nan held an open palm above the tabletop. "At this rate, you'll sell out before tomorrow. We may need to pull an all-nighter and get you restocked. There's still Saturday and Monday to go before the tourists slow down."

Indeed. Monday was bound to be the busiest, and there'd be no work on Sunday. "If I have to work all night, both tonight and on Saturday, I won't complain. I'll be too busy… counting my blessings."

Nan smiled brightly. "It is exciting to have so many customers. I doubt you'll be able to sleep, anyway. I might not, either." Her friend always loved entertaining people and was doing a fine job of it so far today.

Martin strolled toward them with a wooden crate. From the strain of his muscles beneath his short-sleeved shirt, the box was loaded and weighty. He sat it on an empty corner of the table near her. The delicate tinkle of glass against glass followed as sunlight pierced through the golden contents of the mason jars within.

"Where would you like them?" he asked. Perspiration dotted his forehead, causing her to wonder if it was from labor or the strain of being around so many people. "There's three more crates like this one."

She thought quickly about how she might offer him relief without making it obvious. He was trying so hard to support her today. "Can you leave this one here? And maybe take the others to the old cellar round back." The spot was secluded and shaded. She doubted she'd leave the honey there for long but for the time being, it might give Martin a reprieve from the crowd. "I was just about to take a quick lunch break. Wasn't I, Nan?"

She shot her friend a silent plea to agree, although she hadn't planned to stop to eat at all.

"*Ach, ya!* You must take a moment to rest." Nan easily went along with her, and Cassie could've kissed her for understanding.

Cassie placed a hand on Martin's arm. He appeared ready to make his escape to the cellar as fast as he could. "If you don't mind waiting for me there, I'll bring us both a bit of lunch."

"*Denki*, Cass." He wiped his brow with his handkerchief, then worked his way around a huddle of customers who'd just arrived.

"Shoo." Nan flicked the back of her hand at Cassie. "I've got this."

Martin headed back to retrieve the remaining honey from under the shade tree where his uncle had parked his pickup truck. The sun was intense today, as if to declare spring was rapidly transitioning to summer. And he'd noticed the pink of Cassie's skin across her cheeks and the tip of her nose turning red.

A break from the sun would do her good before she burned, so he'd agreed to wait for her. Not that he minded spending a quick lunchtime with her, only that he hoped not to spoil her day with the news his uncle brought.

His day had come close to ruination because of it. A few private moments with Cassie might salvage it, at least in part, until he figured out what to do.

Uncle Titus was waiting for Martin at the truck with the remaining three crates of honey. His back was propped against the driver's-side door, his arms crossed, and his head leaned against the window so that he looked up into the tree from underneath of it.

Martin lifted a crate from the back of the truck, and his uncle came to help with another.

"She wants these last few hauled up to the cellar out back. I can get them. You mentioned going across the way for lunch with *Gammi* Ada." Martin preferred to spend his time with Cassie alone, rather than have his uncle dominate the conversation. He would've felt rude, if he wasn't also sure his grandmother was eager to visit with Titus, her youngest son whom she saw so seldom.

"Alright, then." Titus set the crate back down. "I know you need some time to work out what to do. I can hang around here and visit a couple of days, but I'll have to be going home early on Monday." His uncle clapped a hand on Martin's shoulder. "Just let me know."

"I will," Martin agreed. As much as he dreaded the decision ahead of him, as Titus walked down the driveway to cross the lane.

Martin set the crate he'd picked up on top of the one his uncle had just put down, in order to carry them both at the same time. He'd carry all three at once, but didn't want to risk breaking any of the precious load. This was the last of his supply before this summer's harvest. One he now knew might prove to be the worst since he began, if he didn't act quickly.

After he'd carried his second and final load of honey to the cellar, Cassie came to him from the back of her bakehouse with their luncheon as promised.

"Peanut butter sandwiches." She lifted one, along with a napkin, out of a brown paper satchel. He took it, and she dipped her hand back into the sack. "And an apple."

He accepted the fruit and sat in the grass, leaning against the cool cellar door. She joined him and placed a capped quart-sized jar of lemonade onto the stepping stone, which had long ago been wedged into the space of ground between them.

"Are you alright?" she asked after they'd said thanks for the food and begun to eat.

"If you mean with the crowd, *ya*. Being outdoors helps." He unscrewed the lid from the lemonade jar and chugged a swig, hopeful she wouldn't press further. He had no desire to explain what was bothering him. He'd have to, and sooner than he'd like, but preferably not yet. Today was for

Cassie. "Your bakehouse appears a popular site already. You must be pleased."

She raised an eyebrow but took the bait. "I couldn't have hoped for better. And I couldn't have done it without you."

But she could have. Would have. It had only been a matter of time.

"I'm thankful *Gott* allowed me to be here at the right time, Cass."

"In spite of the fact I messed up your plans to set up your hives and skip out of Promise without being seen." Her lips quirked in a cheeky grin.

"Especially so. I wouldn't have it any other way now." Wholeheartedly, he meant it.

Her smile tipped up slowly, warmly, when she glanced over at him. She held his gaze a moment before taking a crunchy bite out of her apple, then leaned back against the door beside him and sighed.

"Good apple?" he asked.

"A *goot* life." She closed her eyes and ate all the way to the core in that contented manner.

He wished he'd never have to disappoint her, yet knew he would.

Chapter Thirteen

If ever Cassie needed a Sunday as a day of rest, this was the one. Both Friday and Saturday had been busy at the bakehouse. Sightseers from the Blue Ridge Parkway had been a tireless stream through their otherwise sleepy hamlet. And those who were unaware of Cassie's new bakery when they stopped at Weaver's Amish Store became well-informed. Nick and Fern made sure they and their employees mentioned the new bakery to all of their customers. The cars arriving at Cassie's Country Bakehouse didn't slow until after dusk when the traffic along the scenic tour route dwindled to almost nothing.

As expected, she and Nan had worked together for several hours after closing the night before to stockpile more product for Monday's holiday rush. Her *mamm* had also helped, as today was a visiting Sunday and she had been free of her responsibilities of preparing for a church meeting. Zach disappeared, undoubtedly to go out riding with whichever girl he'd chosen for the day. But Martin remained until the bitter end, cleaning the yard of litter, sweeping, mopping and even scrubbing cookie sheets and bread pans.

She watched for him now from the old tire swing that hung in her parents' side yard. From here their gravel lane was fully visible all along its path down the hillside and beyond the dip where it climbed the next hill before curving out of sight to the place where it joined the paved road maintained by the state.

A warm breeze caressed her face as she swung back and forth, admiring the landscape so familiar to her. Fields newly mown and others freshly plowed with sown burrows drawing lines for her eyes to trace as far as she could see. And there, the fullness of a mountain ridge drew a crooked line across the horizon.

Her vision descended back to the road as the swing descended. A dust trail followed Martin's buggy down the far hill as he drove toward her. She waited until he reached the dip in the bottom before jumping to the ground and walked to the mailbox to wait for him.

His blue shirt was pressed, a remarkable difference to his everyday state after trekking through woods and fields for his bees. His hat hid whether he'd combed his hair or not, but she suspected he had. Not that it mattered much. Her heart raced faster either way when he smiled at her and hopped down from the two-seater to stand in front of her.

She'd waited longer than any sensible Amish girl might to go for a ride in a courting buggy with Martin Beiler. And she wasn't feeling anything considered remotely sensible now, either. Not with the way his green eyes pierced hers, his mouth tipped up in a silently tender greeting, and his hand outstretched for hers.

She'd agreed not to worry about what would happen at the end of June when it came time for him to leave. Agreed to wait—which she felt she'd done more than her fair share of already—wait and see what happened. So, she pushed the fear of his leaving as far from her thoughts as possible, took his hand and believed that for once Martin was well and truly courting her.

The effect made her giddy, terrified and delighted all at the same time.

She held her breath as he helped her up. If he kissed her hand again, she might faint. He did not, though his eyes twinkled at her as if he was remembering the last time when he did.

On the buggy floor lay a picnic basket and a blanket alongside his hiking pack, in which he hauled around his beekeeping gear. Was he planning to take her to his hives? Some of her thrill at the moment lessened with the prospect.

"How much walking do you feel up to doing today?" He glanced at her feet. She'd worn her hiking shoes, and he grinned.

"You promised to take me on a tour in search of wild-flowers, remember?" She stretched out a leg and waved a shoe at him. "I came prepared."

With a bump of his shoulder against hers, he answered, "I haven't forgotten. The flora book is in the basket. You've been working so hard, is all. You'll let me know if you get tired?"

Her fatigue had vanished the moment she'd seen him coming down the hill. She very much doubted she'd tire of spending time with Martin any time soon. "*Ya*, I'll let you know."

"I've been scouting new locations for more beeyards. Closer to the parkway, the mountain laurel is thick. Since I have to avoid those flowers, I've been hunting for areas with plenty of other sources of pollen and nectar."

"What's wrong with mountain laurel?" The rhododendron bushes grew enormous in wooded areas and were a key attraction to tourists when in bloom.

"The nectar is poison to honeybees. Bumblebees pollinate the mountain laurel without harm, but honeybees will die from it." The lines that had formed across his brow lessened. "Mostly, honeybees seem to stay away from it, but I want to make sure they have plenty of other sources of food to be on the safe side."

"I didn't know." The confession made her aware yet again of her ignorance about the subject Martin loved.

"I doubt most people do. Bees will forage for their food around about a two-mile radius. So, I'm looking for areas with an abundance of other flowers and as little of the mountain laurel as possible. That's what makes the lavender fields so *goot*. *Vell*, that and the lavender makes a fruity honey folks love." He stopped talking abruptly, although she was sure he'd meant to say more. "Am I boring you?"

"*Nay*, Martin. I want to know." And unlike all the times he'd talked about his bees before, she'd actually listen. She truly regretted she hadn't had the wisdom to do so through all the years he'd shared with her before he left.

Maybe she'd grown a little wiser. Being a friend wasn't all about what the relationship brought to you. A *goot* friendship was a two-sided investment, in which both sought to understand and build up the other. She may never be an expert on bees, but she was capable of learning. And she ought to know more about something so much a part of who he was.

"What is it that you were going to say?" she prodded.

"Zollman's Creek is lined with wild roses, and there's a field close by filled with clover and another with wild strawberries and buttercups. It's an easy trek with plenty of flowers in bloom." He took a second to glance at her, then back to the road. "What do you think?"

"Sounds *wunnerbar* to me." She wrapped her hand through the crook of his elbow without any forethought. As she considered whether she ought to drop her hand back to her lap, Martin transferred the reins into one hand and covered hers with his other. The clear sign that her touch was welcome made her heart soar.

Martin Beiler was courting her. Her ballooning heart might burst.

He slowed the horse to make a turn and cross the creek over a one-lane plank bridge built as far back as a century or more. While the wooden parts of the bridge had likely been replaced several times over, the stone walls on the embankments had weathered decades and floods to remain standing.

The horse's hooves clattered, and the wheels rumbled across the gaps between the boards. All the while she held Martin's arm for the bumpy ride across the bridge, then at the other side, he eased the buggy to a flat shoal on the creek bank, so the horse could drink.

After the horse had her fill, they drove along a dirt trail, no more than two ruts worn into the ground from use by farm equipment. Then, the path wound about a hillside to the clover-laden field Martin had mentioned.

He parked under the shade at the wood line and tethered the horse to a low hanging tree branch, then came back to give her a hand down.

"What would you like to do first?" he asked.

"I'm not hungry." Her family had only just finished lunch before Martin came for her. "Are you?"

He shook his head. "How about a walk, then?"

She agreed, and he strapped his pack on his back before offering her his arm again. Somewhat glad to know he hadn't actually set up any hives here, she felt like she could wander these woods and streams with him all day.

Yet. He hadn't set up beehives here, *yet*. She must be tired, after all, to have just realized what that meant. Because it could only mean he planned to add more hives to his business in Promise.

And that meant he'd be spending more time in Promise, which was more than she'd dare to hope these past weeks. Suddenly, she felt so light of foot she could skip all the way up to the mountain's peak.

Martin had the best of intentions when he'd first suggested bringing Cassie along for a wildflower hunt through the woods. He'd believed he'd have another month to spend with her after they'd pulled off her grand opening. Every day now, he prayed for an open door that might allow him to stay. And he'd assumed that within another month, he'd have a clear direction on what to do.

He had dreams for this beauty of a parcel of land they now traversed. And watching Cassie make her dream for the bakery come true, he'd gained inspiration that he may do the same for his own dreams here. With a profitable summer harvest this year, he could purchase this acreage. Within a few years, the income he gained here might even replace what he made in the valley.

That door had shut in his face with the news Uncle Titus brought to him after his inspection of Martin's beeyards down in the valley.

And now he had to tell Cassie.

He'd pushed the nagging thoughts of it as far back as he could in order to enjoy this last day with her. He shoved them back again. He needed a little longer and the right moment to tell her.

They'd paused to sit on a fallen tree by the water. Cassie held a package of trail mix he kept in his pack for snacking.

"Doesn't this mix come with chocolate pieces?" She

gave the bag a gentle shake looking for the candies he'd already picked out and eaten.

"It does." He waited, knowing what was coming.

"You're meant to eat it all together, not pick out each item individually. Why not just buy a bag of candy or a bag of nuts? That would be easier."

"One bag is easier to lug around, and I like the rest of it, too." Just not all mixed up in his mouth.

She shrugged and popped a cashew into her mouth.

"Save me some chocolate—" she glanced up at him through eyes, as dark and warm as melted cocoa "—in the future."

Did she wish for a future filled with days together as much as he did?

"Are you thirsty?" he asked, while retrieving a canteen of water. He offered it to her first, even though his mouth had gone very dry.

"Denki." She took a long draught and passed it back to him. "What time do you think it is?"

He reached into his pocket until his fingertips connected to the cool silver casing of his pocket watch. He withdrew it, unlatched the clasp and raised the lid. "Almost four."

Her focus zoomed in on the watch. Martin was usually careful—*nay*, always careful—not to open his watch in front of others. As far as he was aware, no one had ever seen the contents hidden inside. He snapped it shut.

"How did you get it—the lock of my hair?"

Cassie watched Martin shove his watch into his pocket. He gulped a swig of water and squirmed as if attempting to find a more comfortable position. She hadn't meant to make him uneasy or pry. But it was her hair, after all.

"I had a picture of you in there at first." He blurted out the admission with haste.

Cassie couldn't hold back the laugh that bubbled out of her. "Wherever did you get a photo? You're becoming more and more mysterious."

He laughed at that, too.

"Maybe you don't remember. I was only eight, so you were about six. A big-name photographer came through here and got a snapshot of you, and the local paper printed it. I cut it out and put it in *Dawdi* Beiler's old watch to keep. Probably the most rebellious thing I ever dared to do."

"I don't suppose Seth put you up to it," she wondered aloud, partly because rules never meant much to Seth's way of thinking, but also because she couldn't imagine that Martin had wanted her picture way back then.

"He can't be blamed for this one. Seth never knew." Martin leaned back and stretched his arms until his hands rested on the ground behind their log seat. He stared up through the trees. "After my *dawdi* passed, I had a tremendous fear of forgetting what he looked like. All I knew was that your photo would ensure I never forgot you."

Her heartbeat tripped on that confession, and she held her breath, hoping he'd explain more. But he was lost in thought and she had to prod. "But you have a snip of my hair, not my image."

He turned his head to her, as though suddenly distracted from something else.

"Ya." He shook his head before staring back at the sky and continuing. "Eli was fit to be tied, as you can imagine—with no imagination required, really. I understand now that it was more than having a stranger take your photo. Tourists do so all the time, and we accept it. Even non-Amish parents would expect their permission to be re-

quired before a photo of a young child was published. But I didn't know all that at eight years old."

"Your *datt*'s wrath put the fear of *Gott* into me. If he ever knew I kept that news clipping in my watch, I'd be toast." He turned his head to make eye contact. "Shunned."

"*Ach*, Martin, you'd not have been shunned for it."

"*Vell*, for sure and certain I was convinced otherwise. So, I had to find another way to remember you." He shrugged, as if that was the end of the story.

He was tired of talking. She knew it. But she couldn't just let him stop before telling her how he managed to come by such a perfect curl of her hair.

"*Un...vass neksht?*"

"What next?" he repeated, stalling.

"*Bitte*, Martin, you can't just end the story there. How did you get my hair?"

"Playing in the creek." His account was growing shorter, either because he was spent of words or didn't want to tell her. "You were searching for crawdads. Concentrating so hard that you didn't notice."

She lifted an eyebrow. "Didn't notice what?"

He twisted sideways to look at her again, then pushed himself back upright so that his arms were free of his weight. Her breath caught in her chest as he leaned toward her and touched the back of her neck right below her prayer *kapp*.

"There," he said without letting his hand drop. "Your curls had come free. So I snipped one with my Swiss Army knife."

"I never knew." Her whisper was so low he mightn't have heard if he wasn't mere inches from her lips.

"Uh-uh." His mouth didn't move with the sound, though his green eyes turned dark as emeralds when she looked back into them.

She kissed him. She was certain he'd silently asked her to, and without any hesitation, she offered up her first kiss. Sweet and perfect and over far too fast.

"Cass." His voice was as tender as his touch, where his hand strayed from the back of her neck to her cheek. "I couldn't forget you."

She rather wished for another kiss, but he stood and hefted his pack over his shoulders. It was time to go, apparently. She brushed the leaves and bits of bark from her skirt, then they began their trek back to the field where the horse and buggy waited.

The silence between them as they rode back to her house grew heavy, unlike their usual peaceful quiet moments. By the pinch of Martin's brow and the occasional grimace that flashed across his expression, he must be rehearsing a rather unpleasant memory or conversation in his mind.

Disappointment on her part might be selfish, but she still wanted to revel in the joy of their first kiss. They hadn't picnicked as she'd supposed they might, but left straight away. And all the while, Martin grew more and more gloomy.

Not a good sign. Not at all.

"Martin?" she asked for his attention.

"Hmm?"

He was about to turn into her parents' drive, and she feared she might lose her opportunity to learn what bothered him if she didn't ask outright.

"Are you upset about our…kiss?" Since she'd been the one to initiate their kiss, she'd begun to wonder if she imagined he'd been an equally enthusiastic participant.

He shook his head rather vigorously and pulled the horse to a halt before turning to face her. "*Nay.* I won't ever be sad or sorry for it. I'll treasure it."

The words thrilled her. She looked up at him as a smile began to turn her lips upward. "I'm glad."

"You won't be, I'm afraid. Not for long." He scratched his elbow, and Cassie felt her smile fade. "I've never broken a promise to you, Cass. Never before…"

She shook her head. He certainly never had, yet she sensed an unpleasant exception coming. Her heart sank.

Martin's shoulders sagged, and he looked away before continuing. "Tomorrow, *Onkel* Titus is leaving early. If I don't go with him, I may lose a substantial number of my hives."

"Why?" The question escaped through a gasp. "What has happened?"

He turned to her then, his eyes sad as he ran his hand down his clean-shaven face. "More than one thing. One colony appears to be struck with an infection. And from my uncle's description, I am afraid it's a bacteria that will spread and potentially wipe out not only my yard but others for miles around. It has to be stopped." He sighed. "I could simply ask Titus to burn the entire beeyard, taking the risk of losing them despite the chance he may be wrong. But there's trouble at some of the other sites, too. Those aren't as serious, but by the time I am done fixing it all, it will be time to begin the harvest. If there's any to collect."

His eyes looked back into hers, silently communicating both pain and indecision. And she knew he'd stay here, if she asked, because he'd promised her three months. He needed her permission to go with a clear conscience.

The choice ought to be simple. Still, she couldn't force the words out that would release him, as easily as she knew they were the right ones to say. "When will you come back?"

"I'll return for the harvest here. It may end up being

the best of this season." He shrugged, and she understood the irony of it, too. "But if I lose a significant harvest...it won't matter anymore."

"Tell me. What won't matter anymore?"

His glance fell to her lips, and her heart seized. "Then, I'm afraid there'll be no more kisses. I'd hoped, Cass. Prayed. But sometimes *Gott* says no."

The pounding in her chest grew painful, as Martin turned away and exited the buggy. Had her dream truly come so close only to be snatched from her so quickly?

When he came around to help her out of the buggy, she took his hand, still unable to say the words outright that would release him from his promise.

Battling the tears she'd promised herself not to shed again, she focused on her feet with extra care not to trip. He let go of her hand, as she slowly looked up and threw herself around him in a tight hug. Finding her voice, she tilted her face close to his ear.

"I understand, this cannot wait. You must leave."

And letting Martin go was the hardest thing she'd ever done.

Chapter Fourteen

Martin had been away from Promise longer now than he'd been able to stay to help Cassie. The two months he'd spent with her had flown too fast. And the two months plus a week since he'd left had been busy from sunup to sundown. The days were longer, literally, and the few scant hours after dark dragged like a lonesome eternity.

He missed her.

Though, by now, he was certain she'd discovered how capable she was without him. He often wondered if their kiss had become a distant memory to her or if she still wished for another, as he'd been sure she did then. It had taken all of his self-control to hold back when she'd looked up at him so sweetly after the precious gift of a kiss she'd given him.

As short and too soon over as the moment had been, he thought of little else on his porch at night watching the fireflies punctuate the humid summer expanse with their lightning-quick bursts of light.

The peepers croaked a fierce racket all the way across the neighbor's hayfield from the watering hole on the other side. Now and then, a bullfrog bellowed, and Martin felt a kinship to the forlorn fellow. And the cicadas' song lulled him to sleep when he climbed, weary souled, into his bed.

He awoke before dawn to a sound akin to the sizzle of

bacon. Groggy, he rolled over, thinking he'd dreamed it, until the aroma reached him, as well. The rustling of pans, the crack of eggs and the telltale grumbling of his brother soon followed.

"No pepper. How come there's no pepper in here, Martin?" Seth fussed, not really expecting an answer, just muttering to himself.

"Where'd you come from?" Martin snuck up behind his brother and enjoyed seeing him jump.

Fork raised and dripping scrambled egg, Seth aimed the utensil at Martin. "Don't do that."

"You're in my house. Unannounced. And woke me up." Martin shot back.

"And... I'm making you breakfast." Implying his labor over the food made up for everything, Seth dropped the fork back into the sink just before egg trickled onto the floor. "What do you eat, anyway? I had to go all the way back down to the nearest twenty-four-hour store to get these eggs and bacon."

"So, where did you come from? All I know is you headed to Florida."

"Yup. That's where I've been, in and around Pinecraft and Sebring, mostly." No explanation for the long silence or any apology for worrying his family. That was just like Seth.

Martin rubbed his temples. "What time did you get here?" Martin must've been out cold not to hear him.

"Round three, but by the time I'd gone back and forth to stock your pantry, I was hungry."

Martin shook his head. "What time is it now?"

"Four-thirtyish." Seth returned to pouring the eggs in a skillet and flipping the strips of bacon. "Don't worry, I'm fixing enough for us both."

And then, Martin supposed, his brother would crash while Martin spent another long day collecting honey. Though he was grateful to have honey to harvest. His uncle had been right about the bacterial infection in one of his hives, and thankfully he'd caught the case of American foulbrood early. The disease was like a cancer, both in the way it could spread and in the fact that the sooner it was detected the better the chance of eradicating it.

He'd been forced to destroy an entire hive yard to prevent the spread and alerted other beekeepers in the area to maintain a close vigil. At this point, he was confident they'd caught the disease early enough to be sure it hadn't spread elsewhere. So while the loss was painful, he knew it could have been far worse.

He'd visited all of his beeyards after that and found nothing else so serious. Some were producing better than others, as expected. And he'd lost a couple to predators. All in all, he still expected to come out with a decent harvest. And with the mountain honey added to his inventory, he couldn't ask for much more.

Or he wouldn't have before he'd started to hope for more. *Nay*, more than hope. He'd been exploring possibilities for making a life back in Promise. And his attempts at wooing Cassie must've been going better than he'd thought.

She'd kissed him, after all. Or they'd just met in the middle. He couldn't tell for sure. He'd been trying not to kiss her, knowing he had to leave. It just happened. And continued to torture him.

Like now.

"You gonna eat or just stand there scratching your head?" Wooden chair legs scraped against the bare floor as Seth scooted up to the table. Next to him was a second plate, piled high with eggs, bacon and toast.

"It's been a while since I ate this *goot*," Martin admitted, though he hated to make his brother's head swell more than it usually was already.

"Let me guess? Since I left, two years ago." There was a challenge in Seth's voice. Sure, he wasn't above boasting, but his eyes twinkled as if he knew there was more to the answer.

Unwilling to take the bait—or discuss his time in Promise—Martin shook his head before bowing it in silent prayer. A tradition his brother openly shunned. He could hear him chewing his bacon beside him.

"At least chew with your mouth closed." Martin stabbed his fork into the eggs on his plate after he finished thanking *Gott* for his food.

"Tell me when you last had a meal as *goot* as this one, then, and I'll try harder not to gross you out." Seth wasn't above boasting or bribery, apparently.

Maybe throwing Seth a tiny morsel of information was worth being able to eat in peace. "Cassie Weaver opened her own bakehouse. I *was* eating plenty *goot*."

"Was—as in you're not anymore? And where is the bakery? I'll make sure to buy from her while I'm here." Seth hadn't bothered to swallow and Martin had to look away.

"Sorry." Seth closed his mouth and swallowed. "I'm starving. Didn't stop to eat, just drove the eleven hours straight through."

Martin dodged the questions that would lead to a discussion about Promise. "Eating with other people doesn't bother me as much as it used to." The sounds and odors of family meals were often an unbearable assault on his sensory system as a child. "You're just a bigger *pikk* than other people."

Seth gave him a playful jab in the arm. "That's for calling

me a pig. But you're the one who mentioned Cassie, so don't try to avoid the subject now." He jumped up and started searching the cabinets. "I know I saw coffee. Aha, there it is. I'll brew an extra strong pot to loosen your tongue. Besides, I'm going to need it to stay awake today."

Seth planned to stay awake after driving all night—that was unexpected. "What are you going to be doing?"

"Helping you, of course." He shrugged and stared, like Martin had asked a ridiculous question. "Now, out with it. And I'm warning you, no tricks. Word travels through Amish circles all the way down to Florida. I'll know if you're leaving stuff out."

Martin sighed. He should have known. Nine weeks was plenty of time for news to circulate through the Amish in all forty-eight states.

"Then why ask?"

"Because I want the Martin version, not the gossip edition."

Fair enough. Martin would appreciate the same courtesy. And before he began, he told his brother he expected a full account of Seth's own in return.

Sunday church meeting was held in her *Dawdi* Dan's barn that morning, and Cassie was distracted. This was the ninth Sunday since the last one she'd spent with Martin.

She ought to stop counting.

Maybe she would stop if she couldn't see his courting buggy through the barn window with the view across to the Beiler's where he'd parked it. Maybe she would stop if the lavender fields weren't past their peak, which meant the honey was also sure to be ready for harvest. Or maybe she would stop if she quit visiting the beeyard behind the bakehouse to watch his bees with her brother's hunting binoculars or read one of the books Martin left behind.

But most of all, she knew that if she hadn't kissed him, she wouldn't be counting the weeks until she might get another one.

She knew he'd return for his honey. Martin always kept his word. Only he'd also left his pocket watch with the lock of her hair. Did that mean he didn't want to be reminded of her? And if so, then she was a *dummkopf* to still be pining over him.

After the service and the meal, all the *youngies* enjoyed the time to visit with each other. But today, Cassie dreaded mingling with the other single women. Nan, to be precise, who'd informed her all about the lavender honey in a whisper as they walked into the service.

As much as she loved her friend, the last thing Cassie wanted to hear was how much Nan knew about the state of Martin's honey harvest in Reuben's fields. So she skirted around the edge of the barn to avoid the group gathering nearby. Making her way to the farmhouse, she noticed Fern on the porch with Cassie's *mamm*, each cradling one of the new twins in their arms.

Fern wasn't likely to pepper her with questions about Martin, not now, with two *bopplis* consuming all her energy and attention. And her *mamm* was never intrusive, only listened when Cassie needed to talk.

Right now, Cassie preferred to talk about almost anything other than herself, Martin Beiler, bees or honey.

"*Datt* was looking for you, Cassie." Her *mamm* looked up from the sweet *boppli*'s face for a moment. Cassie wasn't sure which twin she held, Maria or Ellen. "He's inside."

Too late to change course, though she might prefer to navigate a discussion with Nan over one with her *datt*,

Cassie resigned herself to whatever was coming. Eli Weaver didn't summon you to shoot the breeze. He meant to get down to the very heart of whatever matter brought you to his attention.

She found him rummaging through *Dawdi* Dan's tackle box and holding his pole.

"Hello, Cassie," he said as he hooked a lure to the end of his line. "How about a little stroll?"

It wasn't an actual question, so she merely nodded.

He peered over his shoulder at the corner behind him. "Would you like to take a pole?"

"Um, sure." She was a terrible fisher, even when handling live bait wasn't a requirement. "I can try, I guess."

A pole was chosen, a lure attached, and they left through the back door to head to the creek through the apple orchard. The fruit was still green, though the branches were heavily laden with the promise of a large harvest.

There was always something soothing about walking through the orchard. She felt less and less anxious as they continued passing through the trees. Her *datt* whistled a tune she felt sure he made up as he went along.

Perhaps it was all the fond times their family had spent in the orchard that made it so calming and special. She ought to come here more often, she thought before another idea came to mind.

"Do you think *Gammi* Weaver would like to sell her apple butter at the bakery? Uncle Nick's Amish supplier provides him with the large quantities the store needs. But for the bakery, apple butter would be a novelty item."

"Can't hurt to ask her. I'm sure she'd be delighted that you considered her." Her *datt*'s long strides made conversation difficult, as she had to take two steps for each of his

He slowed as they neared the creek and continued walking in the opposite direction of the current, which would soon wind around to the Beiler's property deeper in the woods. Finally, he paused at the bottom of a hill near a bend in the stream, where pebbles and stone had washed ashore to create a wider shore, and the flow pooled away from the babbling rush farther across the water.

There was nowhere to sit without ruining their Sunday best, and he made no attempt to cast his line but rubbed his beard before speaking. "Martin asked for permission to court you before he knew he'd be leaving. And I gave my blessing, believing he'd proven his intent to stay."

Cassie startled at the abrupt opening of the subject. Her *datt* was often direct, but this revelation was confusing, if straight to the point. "He asked… Martin asked *you*? I didn't know."

"I suspected not." His response was filled with care.

She hadn't even been sure Martin was courting her until he bought that buggy, and even then, it had taken some time to sink in. "Everything started…and ended so fast."

Her father's hand gently cupped her elbow, and she looked up into his compassionate gaze. "*Dochter*, I've known since both of you were but *kinner* that the day would come when the two of you would have to decide whether your paths were to continue side by side. I prayed for wisdom to know when the time was right—that you were both mature enough to choose for yourselves. And I've agonized over the past weeks, whether I made a mistake."

"You mean in giving your consent?" *Ach*, but she knew he hadn't done so in haste. He'd taken all these years to allow a man near her.

He nodded. "But I don't believe I have. As much as a father would like to make all things easy for his child, it is not possible in this world. If Martin's hives hadn't become infected, things may have gone the way we all hoped."

Was he saying that he had been hopeful things would work out for her and Martin? Her head swam just thinking about it. "But *Datt*, Martin was afraid of you. And even I... even I thought you were opposed to all the matchmaking and secret courtship rumors."

"Cassie, I was opposed only before you were ready. And Martin, he also needed to come into his own." His hand moved from her elbow to her shoulder with a gentle pressure and reassurance. "I would only let you go to a man worthy of you. And I still believe Martin could be that man." He looked at something beyond her and dropped his hand back to his side.

Martin was the one, she wanted to blurt out. But the chance she'd finally been given had not worked out, and her heart ached with the severest disappointment.

"Why don't you stay here awhile and think about it? You know your way back, *ya*?" Her *datt* was already stepping back into the trees the way they had come.

She nodded, relieved to have a moment to collect her thoughts.

To mourn alone...

Her childhood friendship turned adolescent infatuation had grown into something far deeper. And now she'd learned that she'd been closer than she'd dared to hope of grasping a *wunnerbar* dream.

But it was to remain a dream. She felt the smooth round metal of Martin's pocket watch inside her apron. He'd chosen to leave her behind, for *goot* this time.

Martin hadn't considered the possibility of coming upon Eli and Cassie Weaver near his favorite fishing hole, not on a church Sunday so near to mealtime. He'd driven Seth's truck to the bakehouse, where he'd parked out of sight and walked to his parents' house. It was a long hike, and he'd arrived too late for church service and meant to go off by himself until the gathering next door had dwindled.

He also supposed he'd have more time before facing Eli Weaver or Cassie and considered heading back before Eli spotted him. Then, he knew he had to face him. He'd rather not complicate the uncertainty of his reception from the minister by fleeing like a coward. Not after he'd left town, mere days after he'd given his blessing for Martin to court Cassie. Of course, Martin had a *goot* reason for leaving then, but he had none to run off now.

As Martin continued in their direction, Eli walked away. He stepped into the woods, leaving Cassie and sending Martin a barely perceptible nod and a slight raise of his hand in silent greeting.

However, Cassie hadn't seen Martin yet, or her *datt*'s signal to him. He could still bypass her.

Nay, he could not. Nor did he truly desire to. There was no one in the world he'd rather be with this afternoon. The trouble was, he still didn't have answers for the questions she was bound to ask him.

She squatted, hovering above the ground and tucking her skirt behind her bent knees so as not to soil it. Her pole lay beside her. She picked up a stone and rubbed her thumb over it, then dropped it and chose another. This one must have been satisfactory, because she drew her arm back and aimed the rock before releasing it to skip across the water.

He was close now and called out to prevent frightening her. She dropped another rock she'd just chosen and stood facing him.

"Hello, Martin." She rubbed her palms together in front

of her to clean off the dirt. If she was surprised to see him, he couldn't tell. Her expression was placid, and he wasn't able to interpret whether she was happy to see him, which probably meant she wasn't.

He took a deep breath and closed the remaining gap between them, careful not to get too close. "It's *goot* to see you."

She looked down at her feet, then turned to face the water. "I suppose you came to harvest your honey, then."

Nay, she was not happy to see him.

And he'd never been so disappointed in his life.

Chapter Fifteen

"Seth came to see me." Cassie wasn't sure what she'd expected Martin to say, but not that. "He's doing better, I think. He's finishing up the honey harvest for me. Not here, of course. He's doing that down in the valley, so I could come back and…"

"Nan said the lavender honey is ready." Her tone was curt and the interruption rattled him. She winced. She hadn't meant to be rude, only to avoid embarrassing herself by throwing her arms around him the way she wanted to.

"How would Nan know?" His expression was perplexed.

"She's a sudden expert on all things lavender." Cassie shrugged.

"Hmm," he muttered. "Or all things Reuben."

Cass couldn't help but laugh, and the tension between them broke. His green eyes sparked, and his smile broke free, making him appear as handsome as ever.

"You must have a *goot* harvest, after all, if Seth is needed to help." She smiled back because she was determined to be happy for him, even if his success down in the valley kept him from Promise—from her.

"I lost one of my best producing yards."

She was sorry for that, but couldn't find a way to say so, since he didn't appear sad in the least. If anything, the way he was looking at her was making her feel a little speechless.

"But the *goot* news is," he went on, "there was little other damage, and the harvest here could more than make up for what I lost."

"*Ya*, I expect so." Cassie always knew Martin kept his promises, but he'd kept some secrets, too. "Reuben's wild bee swarm wasn't the only one you caught, so I discovered."

He shoved his hands in his pockets and gave her a sheepish look. "I wasn't keeping it from you. You were busy and…you don't like bees, Cass. And *ya*, I did order some queen bees to give some of those new colonies a healthy start. I reckon Nan sniffed that out, huh?"

Cassie didn't know anything about the queen bees, but Nan likely had found out about them and thought to pull that prank. "Probably. All I know is that I've discovered forty-four of your ten-frame hives all over Promise."

Martin sputtered. Whether she'd shocked him by knowing his hives were ten-frames or by the fact that she'd ventured close enough to find them and count them, she was thoroughly enjoying the surprised look on his face.

Once he'd closed his mouth, his lips turned up in a sideways grin, and she came dangerously close to thinking about that kiss again.

She looked down at the pole she'd forgotten on the ground and retrieved it as a distraction.

"Did you want to go fishing?" He nodded at the pole.

"Not really." The admission had slipped out before she could think of how ridiculous she must look out here alone with a fishing pole and no intention to use it. She ought to take her pole and herself back to the house, before he asked what she was doing out here.

"You never enjoyed fishing," he said instead. "I reckon not everything is changing."

Like her knowing about bees. Or did he mean something else?

"Is there a singing, tonight?" Now, that was something new, maybe even bigger than her learning about bees. He'd never cared about a singing before.

"Why? I mean, *ya*, of course there is. But why do you ask?"

"Would you like to go with me?" His eyes met hers, full of sincerity.

Sweet Martin. All she could manage was a nod as she held a hand over her heart in an attempt to keep it from flying right out of her chest.

He stepped back from her, creating more room to breathe between them, but not losing eye contact. "I'll pick you up around six, if that's okay. Will you be at home or at your grandparents' house still?"

"I'll be at home." The words squeaked past her excitement, which was building to a crescendo.

She would've remained at her grandparents' house all afternoon because that's where the singing was to be held. But she'd find a way home, just so Martin had to drive all the way to get her and escort her properly. She'd waited far too long for him to take her to a Sunday singing to let him off the hook too easily.

He turned to go, then whirled back around. "Cass, have you seen my *Dawdi* Beiler's watch? I've searched everywhere and thought I must have left it here, but it wasn't in my upstairs room at the bakehouse, either."

If she returned it to him now, he'd see what she had done. She was nervous to see his reaction when he opened it and discovered what she'd placed inside. She hadn't meant for him to see the image she'd hidden behind her lock of hair but knew she couldn't wait to return it to him. The worry on his face was so acute, her heart pinched. The watch was truly a treasure to him.

She pulled the timepiece from her apron and handed it to him. "You left it."

He didn't ask why she had it in her pocket, only appeared greatly relieved to get it back. "*Denki*, Cass. I couldn't stand to think I'd lost something so precious…and not only the watch, you understand."

She wasn't sure she could unpack all the implications of that statement. She swallowed. "You're welcome."

He pocketed the watch without looking inside, then waved goodbye. "I don't want to be late. See you at six."

"*Ya*, I'll see you then." She waved back.

Perhaps Martin hadn't chosen to forget about her, after all.

And her *datt* had been doing his best to look out for both Cassie and Martin all along. She had to wonder what else she'd been mistaken about and what was going to surprise her next.

She watched Martin walk along the creek toward his fishing hole until he was out of sight. Once she was sure he couldn't see or hear her, she released a happy squeal and tiptoe danced in a circle.

Ach, but she'd waited ever so long for this.

Martin didn't dare to hope he could just pick right back up where he and Cassie had left off, but she'd agreed to go out with him that evening, so he took heart.

Business had to wait until Monday. And until he could settle some of those matters, he didn't know what, if anything, he could offer Cassie yet. But she'd seemed willing to enjoy some time together, which was as much as he could hope for, right now.

He lost interest in fishing not long after he arrived at his favorite spot and turned back to seek out his *datt* and Eli Weaver. Seth, whose advice was not always golden, had given him a few ideas worth pursuing, but he wanted his *datt*'s advice first and then required Eli's permission to make it all work.

Seth had always been one to fight for what he wanted, along with how and when he wanted it, which was usually right away. Whereas Martin let life happen and dealt with it the best he could as it came. Probably a better balance existed somewhere in between. And Martin had decided now was his time to give things a push in the direction he wanted to go.

Being away from Cassie had left him sure of a few things. He didn't want to be apart from her longer than necessary ever again. Promise, he'd also discovered, was more home to him than anywhere else. Seth might not be able to find happiness here, but Martin had. So, he'd do whatever it took to stay in Promise and be with Cassie.

He didn't have it all figured out, and much was beyond his control. So, he'd do all he could and trust the rest to *Gott*. That was all no guarantee that he'd get what he wanted in the end. But also unlike his brother, Martin still believed *Gott* always did what was for their best.

"What about autism?" Seth had asked.

And Martin's answer was still yes. Even with autism, *Gott* worked all things out for Martin's good.

He exited the woods right behind his parents' house and away from the church crowd, using more caution to remain unseen than he had before. Somehow, finding Eli with Cassie near his fishing hole seemed like too much of a coincidence. Although he couldn't fathom why Eli would have taken her to him.

Perhaps the timing was all coincidental. Either way, he didn't want to risk being seen again just yet. He wanted to share the news about Seth with his parents privately. If he got dragged into a conversation elsewhere, the subject might be difficult to avoid. His *mamm* especially would appreciate hearing the news directly from Martin.

Both of his parents were in the family room, dozing in their chairs. Fern, too, was asleep on the couch. She lay on her side with an arm hanging limply over the edge of the cushion, as if she'd passed out while watching her two girls, who were nestled side by side on a blanket on the floor.

Somehow, he knew he'd be in serious trouble if he woke the *bopplis*. So, he tiptoed around Maria and Ellen to the rocking chair, the last available seat, contemplating a Sunday afternoon nap himself. Taking care not to make a sound, he withdrew the pocket watch to check the time.

The cool, smooth exterior was soothingly familiar. He often fiddled with the watch for grounding when his nerves were on edge, and he'd almost panicked when he thought he might've lost it. He lifted the lid and realized something wasn't the same. The lock of Cassie's hair was at a different angle. Looking closer, he saw an image, a silhouette type, underneath. The shadowed shape was small and partially covered by the locket taped to it, but he was fairly confident the drawing was of him.

He closed his eyes, but there'd be no nap for him. His blood was pounding through his veins too fast for sleep. Cassie had placed his image in the watch. She'd put the two of them together, at least symbolically. He certainly believed they belonged together in a very real sense.

But even if he was reading more into this than she'd intended, one thing was sure. She hadn't forgotten him while he was gone, after all.

Being wrong wasn't usually so thrilling. And he couldn't help but wonder where else his assumptions had been so far off the mark. And all of a sudden, he had more motivation to push for what he wanted than ever before.

Chapter Sixteen

Each day of the week since Martin took Cassie to the Sunday singing, he'd also shown up at her house to drive her to work. This morning had been the first exception because he had family business to attend to.

Cassie thought that sounded a bit mysterious but hadn't prodded. He'd tell her when he wanted her to know, and she was fine with that. Curious maybe, but fine—a sentiment that seemed to follow her all week. The world felt right with Martin back in it.

He'd moved his things out of the bakehouse for appearance's sake, he'd explained. Now that they were courting, well and truly, he didn't want folks to get the wrong idea about him living in her bakery. So, he stayed across the lane with his *Gammi* Ada, which kept him closer than all the way at his parents' house.

Zach and Nan had each been working part-time for her for weeks, so her *datt*'s concerns about her being alone were no longer an issue. And now, she puzzled whether the whole objection had been some convoluted matchmaking ploy all along.

She shook her head. Even her *datt* couldn't have arranged for all of the pieces to fall together the way they had. *Nay*, *Gott* was at work. She just knew it. And she would have to trust Him with the rest of her story. *Please Gott, let it include Martin.*

She pulled the last of the morning's bread from the oven and tapped the tops, which made a hollow thump. *Ya*, they were done and ready for the cooling rack.

The bell above the bakehouse entrance rang, which she supposed was Zach by the heavy clomping up the stairs. He never missed an opportunity to visit the washroom. The store hadn't even opened yet. There was no one here to impress but her.

Ach, but there might be a pretty girl at work in Weaver's Amish Store. Mystery solved. He'd be taking the already cooled and bagged loaves down to the store for *Onkel* Nick to sell. The rest would go on her own shelves after they'd cooled enough to package.

Martin had brought her some lavender honey as soon as he'd collected his first jars on Monday. Her bread alongside his honey had become the bakehouse's top sellers this week. In fact, she prepared extra loaves that morning for the Saturday rush.

More plodding. Down the stairs this time.

Cassie took her attention off her task this time and turned to see her brother. "They're all ready for you." She pointed over her shoulder to the racks of bread.

Zach hefted the first tray off the storage rack. "By the way, have you been paying any attention to what *Datt*'s been up to lately?" He paused, leaning the edge of the tray against the countertop beside her. "You seem oblivious to anything other than Martin at the moment. But—"

"Hey," she interrupted. "Look who's talking. Do you ever think of anything other than girls?"

He smirked, then raised a hand while carefully keeping the bread balanced. "Hold off there, now. I didn't mean to make it a competition." His grin widened. "Besides, we know who'd win."

"You're impossible." She popped him with the corner of her tea towel. "So what is *Datt* up to?"

Zach looked around as if someone might overhear, and Cassie refrained from rolling her eyes at his dramatics. Her brother spoke in a low voice. "You know how he can get busy making rounds to all the families in the *g'may*."

"*Ya*, I know." She made a point of speaking at a normal volume. "He makes those visits to settle any grievances and assure we are all in unity in the weeks before our communion and foot-washing services." Those came twice a year. Once in early spring and again in the fall. Reluctantly, she considered whether Zach might have a point. "But it's the wrong time of year."

"See, I knew you hadn't been paying attention, because it's odd, *ya*?"

She nodded, slowly, still unsure if this was something she ought to worry about.

"Not only is it a strange time of year for so much visiting, while crops are coming in for harvest and so much work needs to be done, I've noticed another peculiar thing."

Perhaps she should worry. "What's that?"

Zach leaned in closer, his eyebrows raised as though he was alarmed. "He's been going round to all our non-Amish neighbors, as well."

"*Vass?* Zach, you're trying to fool me. There's no time for your nonsense. The bakehouse opens in thirty minutes, and I need you back here to help." She was about to give him another harmless swat with the towel, but he wasn't laughing at the joke. The seriousness on his face stopped her. Maybe he didn't believe the ridiculousness he was spouting, but he was concerned about something. "You're not kidding."

"*Nay*, I am not. I'm worried. I never thought our *datt* would be one of those Amish ministers who've gone rogue. I don't want to end up on the news. Zach Weaver, son of the out-of-control Amish man."

"Stop, Zach. When you go on like that, how can I take you seriously? You should just ask him. Talking about it behind his back isn't going to solve anything. You know he must have a reason. We ought to believe in him enough to know it's a *goot* one." She had no reason not to give their *datt* the benefit of the doubt, although she couldn't imagine what he was up to. And what was wrong with Zach that he'd jump to such conclusions?

"This is why I detest gossip. What are you thinking, *bruder*?"

"What I'm thinking, *schwester*," Zach said as he hefted the load of bread back into both arms, "is that you're the one who needs to do the asking."

"Zachariah Weaver." She used his full name on purpose.

"Don't worry. I won't be spreading any rumors. You know me better than that. But ask him, Cassie. I really think *you* should." Then he called over his shoulder, "I saw him walking into Ada Beiler's cottage not five minutes ago. Maybe he'll stop by here, next."

He was gone in a wink, leaving her to wonder how she'd broach such a subject with her father. And what was he doing down at Ada Beiler's place? That's where Martin was taking care of his family business.

She held her head to soothe the ache beginning to throb behind her eyes. What in the world was her father up to now?

"Welcome, Eli." Ezekiel Beiler greeted the minister and motioned toward the sitting area just inside *Gammi* Ada's cottage where Martin sat with his grandmother, as well as his *mamm*, brother and uncle. "Have a seat, if you'd wish. Would you like something to drink?"

"Don't bother, Ezekiel. I'm fine." Eli spoke kindly, and although a cushioned wingback had been spared for him, he sat in one of the wooden dining table chairs Martin had brought into the room for extra seating.

Seth didn't hesitate to move into the comfortable chair. Martin's brother never did boast of being humble, and no one ever accused him of meekness, either. He was here, though, when he'd most likely prefer to be almost anywhere else. And Martin loved him all the more for it.

Martin had invited everyone here. He'd almost asked Cassie, as well. It would have felt right to have her with him. And if things went as he hoped and prayed, then what was done in this room would have a lasting impact on her, too. But those dreams had yet to come true. And for now, being in a situation like this would only have made her uncomfortable.

As it was, everyone else in the room seemed to be wondering why they were here. They all seemed a little uneasy. Except *Gammi* Ada. This kind of thing was what she lived for. She rocked contentedly directly across from him. His parents occupied a love seat, and Seth sat in the wingback chair, which left Eli, Titus and Martin in the dining chairs, all in a vaguely oval arrangement.

"Martin, *liebling*, you've got us all gathered. Why don't you go ahead and tell us what this is all about?" His *gammi*, never shy or at a loss for words, beamed at him.

Feeling suddenly envious of her gift for saying whatever was on her mind, Martin stumbled at his prepared speech.

Seth cleared his throat and spoke in an undertone to Martin. "May I?"

Martin shook his head. As much as Martin appreciated

Seth's willingness to speak for him, he had to do this himself. "I've got it," he answered. He cleared his throat and prayed for the words he'd prepared to come out intelligibly.

"I would like to move back to Promise. Permanently. Cassie doesn't know. Not yet." That seemed very important to say, all of a sudden, and he thought maybe he should have asked her to come after all. Would she be hurt that he'd told everyone here before he told her?

"We can keep a confidence," Eli assured him. That probably was one of a minister's specialties, he supposed.

Martin made the mistake of looking at his *mamm*. She was tearing up. Seeing Seth and having Martin make this announcement might be too much for one day. But she nodded at him. "Go on, *bitte*."

How had he only managed a sentence or two so far? This was not going the way he'd rehearsed in his head. He cleared his throat once more.

Seth stood up. "I've offered to purchase Martin's business down in the valley. That means that Martin will be able to build his business here. Of course, he'll also be wanting to join the church." Seth speared Eli with a look, as if he dared him not to allow such a thing. "I myself won't be moving back to Promise, but I'd like to be close enough to visit. Who knows, *Mamm*, I may find a nice Mennonite girl and get married. I'd have to be close enough to bring your future grandchildren to see you."

Great. Now *Mamm* was crying. Their *datt* put an arm around her shoulder. "There, there."

Thankfully, Seth had enough sense to sit back down.

Martin glanced at Eli. The minister gave him a very slight nod, whether of understanding or a nudge to go on, he was unsure. And he had no time to decide before his *gammi* took the floor.

"Since the waterworks have begun, I may as well make my own announcement." *Gammi* spoke loud enough to drown out anything else. "I'm giving the cottage to Martin."

Martin's head spun with the sudden change of subject. And Uncle Titus's eyes rounded. A year ago, *Gammi* announced she was selling her cottage and going to live with Titus. And she had moved in with Titus's family for a short while. Then, as soon as her little trick got Fern and Nick together, she came back.

"Where will you go?" Titus's voice was laced with caution.

"Florida."

Seth laughed. "*Gammi*, you'll take Pinecraft by storm. You'll love it."

Martin's *datt* and Titus weren't laughing. Each of her sons stared at each other as if to say, "I didn't know, did you?" But Martin knew one thing for sure. No one was going to contradict her.

A throat cleared with the authority that could quiet an entire assembly for prayer. All heads turned to Eli.

"Martin, how about getting us back to the topic at hand?"

He had to think, to recall where he'd left off. "I, um, haven't told Cassie because I'm not sure it will work out."

"Nonsense. Of course, it will." *Gammi* rocked her chair a little harder, while the others waited for him to explain.

His elbow itched, and he really wished Cassie was here now. She'd keep him centered. "It's going to take a couple of years to build a business here like I have down the mountain. I can't even predict if enough farmers will welcome a beekeeper in Promise. And then there's the complication of traveling long distances up here. I can't spread my bee-yards out as far and wide as I did up and down the valley with the use of *Onkel*'s truck."

Finally, part of his rehearsed speech paid off. Everyone seemed to understand what he'd said.

Eli was stroking his beard, then he made eye contact. And for the first time, his gaze didn't scare Martin. "And what else is standing in your way?"

Now he was finally getting to the reason he'd asked Eli to come. Otherwise, he'd have kept the matter in the family.

"I'd want to join the church." He looked at Eli directly. Even though Seth had already spoken for him, Martin needed to say so for himself. "I don't expect an answer now, but I'd like to know if there's no chance. Because that would change…everything." He hoped Cassie's *datt* understood that he'd never ask Cassie to leave Promise or marry him outside of the church. But his words were too spent to explain something so deeply personal and definitely off limits before he talked to her himself.

Remarkably, the room remained still as Eli rubbed his beard and pondered on what Martin had said. Then Eli clapped the palms of his hands around his knees with a sense of finality before he spoke. "Monday. You'll have your answers on Monday. Make sure you are at the bakehouse all day, *ya*?"

Martin nodded in agreement.

"*Vell*, then, I'm sure the rest of the discussions here do not require my assistance." Eli stood. "Perhaps our paths will cross tomorrow when I visit my parents." He was addressing Martin's *mamm* and *datt*. Then, to Titus and Seth, he said, "*Gott* be with you."

Martin rose to get the door, then spoke as he opened the door for Cassie's father. "*Denki* for coming Eli…and for considering my request."

"Monday," he replied, as if Martin might forget. Then

he stepped outside, put on his hat and walked down the footpath.

No doubt, he'd cross the street to go see Cassie. Which was exactly what Martin planned to do as soon as he escaped the circus already resuming in his *gammi*'s sitting room.

"Your *bruder* was born to keep me humble." Cassie's *datt* massaged the back of his neck. "Or put me in an early grave."

"Here, *Datt*." Cassie pushed a giant cinnamon roll in front of him. "And a glass of *kald melka*."

He drank the milk first. And Cassie wished she hadn't listened to Zach. She didn't think her father deserved any more headaches than he already dealt with on a daily basis.

He set down the glass and wrapped the sweet bun in a napkin. "I'll take this with me. If I ruin my lunch, I'll have to answer to your *mamm*." He winked, and she handed him a paper bag. "If Zach paid more attention to detail, he'd have deduced that I haven't been visiting random houses but farmers. *Ya*, both Amish and non-Amish, that part is true. But the results are a surprise. Can you trust me until Monday?"

"I always trust you, *Datt. Vell*, mostly always." She had certainly doubted his intentions concerning Martin just a short time ago. But wait until she got ahold of Zach.

"I know that look." He tapped her chin. "Forgive your brother. He's done no actual harm. I have a hunch he knows more than he's letting on. And in his way, he's looking out for you."

The bell alerted them a customer was in the store.

"See you later and *denki* for the cinnamon bun." He slipped out through the storage room.

She turned to attend to the customer, but it was Martin who had come into the store. No one else. He looked a touch frazzled, yet expectant.

"Are we alone?" he asked.

The way he asked made her very glad of the answer, as if he had something special in mind. "Nan hasn't arrived yet. Zach is helping Uncle Nick, and *Datt* just left."

He came closer. "So, we are alone."

"Ya." She noticed he didn't look frazzled anymore. "You look…"

"Happy to see you?" He grinned, and she found it contagious, smiling right back at him.

"Are you? I was going to say—" she pressed a finger to her lips "—hopeful."

"Close." He laughed. "If you'd said that I look like I can't wait much longer to kiss you again, you'd have been exactly right."

She felt her cheeks warm with a blush, but did her best to appear unaffected. "I had wondered." How long she could play this game? Because her heart might give out. "Why haven't you?"

Her breathing may have stopped, along with her heart, as he took her hands, holding them gently together in his own. Game over. She couldn't pretend anything now. Her feelings had to be written all across her face.

"I can't make you any promises, Cass," he said, and she thought he may kiss her hand as he'd done before. He didn't. "Maybe after Monday."

"Wh-what's Monday?" She pulled her hands back, attempting to return her breathing and heart rate to normal.

"I don't know yet." He stepped back. "But we are going to find out. Be ready."

The doorbell tinkled again, and this time a customer came in.

"Welcome." She greeted a middle-aged couple who seemed to be tourists. "I'll be right with you."

Martin was leaving through the kitchen, so she hurried to him. "Can you stay a little longer?"

"I think I better go," he said, then spotted the hot cinnamon buns still in the baking pan.

"Take one with you." She handed him a spatula to remove one from the pan.

"Is it a Martin Special?" His eyebrow lifted. "Because these favors of yours get me into a whole peck of trouble."

"*Vell*, now, that is up to you. It could become one..." It was her turn to make him nervous. "If you make me wait much longer."

"Two days, Cass. I think we'll make it." He accepted the cinnamon bun without taking his eyes off of her. "Although it won't be easy."

He shoved a bite in his mouth, then picked up the rest to go.

"Monday," he said like a promise, as she left him to help her customers. And she began to anticipate the coming week more than anyone had ever looked forward to a Monday before.

Chapter Seventeen

Martin hitched the horse to his courting buggy and headed out to pick up Cassie before dawn on Monday morning. The time of day wasn't unusual, not for the Amish, and especially not for a baker. Yet Martin knew this was no ordinary day.

Eager to see Cassie, he eased his buggy onto the road with the headlamps lit.

Being early risers was one thing he and Cassie had in common. He was slow to make a decision, while she charged ahead. She was naturally empathetic, whereas he struggled to understand the feelings of those around him. She couldn't stand to wait. He hated to hurry.

But beekeepers and bakers alike rose before the sun. Did he dare hope they'd continue to do so together for a lifetime?

He'd seen Eli speaking with the bishop, elders and deacons one by one the day before. And though he wouldn't know the outcome of those conversations until the minister came to tell him, he'd awoken with a peace that today held good news for him.

But joining the church was only one hurdle he had to jump before he could take his relationship with Cassie to the next level. He had to be sure he could make a living here, too. How Eli planned to give him an answer on that point was still a great mystery to him.

If *Gott* saw fit to grant him a lifetime with Cassie by his side, he figured their differences would balance them. And the ways in which they were alike would ground them.

Ya, that's how he felt with Cassie—grounded. The stimulations all around that set his nerves abuzz eased with her understanding in his life. With her, just her presence, too. That was when he was at his best. She was his place to belong.

Today, he prayed, he could finally tell her so.

As usual, when he reached the end of her parents' drive, Cassie was waiting for him at the mailbox. It always made him feel as if she couldn't wait to see him, which only bolstered his courage.

This morning, she didn't wait for him to get out to help her. She might've jumped in without him coming to a full stop if she could. He smiled. This was one day when he felt a kinship with her desire to hurry. Eli hadn't given away much, but Martin doubted he'd have him wait with Cassie, if he expected to bring bad news.

"Time passes at the same rate, whether you hurry or not, you know, Cass," he teased.

"That's not true." The seat bounced as she settled in beside him. "I can verify that yesterday was the slowest Sunday on record."

"Oh, how's that?" His curiosity peaked.

"Didn't you feel it? Time stopped, right about noon. It took four days off my life waiting for this morning." Her face was all shadows in the predawn, but try as she might to keep a serious tone, the lilt in her voice gave away her silliness.

He laughed out loud. "If you didn't work so hard to hurry

through the hours, you might discover that the time actually passes faster."

"So, you admit it." She bumped her shoulder against his. "Time doesn't flow at a steady rate."

She'd stumped him there, without a ready answer. He laughed again.

"Maybe, Cass. Maybe you're right." He added scientific thinker versus dreamer to their list of opposites. "And I hate to disappoint you, but I have no idea what is happening today. All I know is your *datt* asked me to be at the bakehouse all day. It may be a huge letdown." He prayed not.

"You mean I may have to wait all day?"

He couldn't very well take his eyes off the road long enough to see her expression. "Are you angry, teasing or pouting?"

"Pouting."

Maybe he shouldn't have mentioned anything about today in the first place, just shown up as Eli had asked. All he'd done was make her miserable. But she looped her arm through his, and they rode in silence all the way to the main road. Though not true silence. The birds were waking and the frogs still croaked loudly. Nary a car passed them, while the horse's shoes clicked a steady rhythm.

"Martin?"

"Hmm."

"Don't you at least know a bit of why *Datt* would ask you to wait at the bakehouse? You never explained much. Other than to imply that maybe you'd kiss me again." Her breath hitched, as if she'd spoken without forethought. And while his heart rate zoomed at the mention of another kiss, she whispered, "Will you?"

The loaded question tempted him to pull over and kiss her right then and there. Would he be able to stay away from Cassie if things didn't go the way he hoped today? He wasn't sure he had enough willpower, if *Gott* put him to such a test.

"Martin, what are you thinking? You haven't answered me." Her voice was soft, gently prodding him for a response.

"That's two questions. Do I get to pick which one I want to answer?" He'd rather return to her question about what to expect from her *datt* than talk about kissing. He only had so much strength, after all.

"*Nay*. Answer both, *bitte*." She knew she was pushing his limits and sounded as if she was enjoying it.

"I explained to your *datt* that I want to return to Promise. Come back to say." This wasn't how he'd planned to tell her he wanted to stay in Promise, but she deserved to know. And he sure as shooting wasn't going to spoil their next kiss by stealing one here. *Nay*, that was worth waiting for.

Her hand had squeezed his arm, but then she'd gone absolutely still. Stranger still, she'd gone quiet. After all the years she'd pleaded for him to come back, wasn't she pleased?

"Cass?"

He felt her posture snap straight beside him.

"Pull over, Martin Beiler," she demanded.

"I can't just pull over. It's half-dark and dangerous." Even with his battery powered lights and reflectors, there wasn't anywhere safe to pull to the side of this country road.

"Well, I can't hug you while you're driving," she huffed.

He felt a smile spread across his face. "You could come closer."

She snuggled up under his arm. Not the safest, but definitely the coziest solution.

"When were you going to tell me? Do you know how hard I've prayed for this? I mean, I also tried to trick you into staying, and beg you into staying, and when nothing worked, I had to wait for *Gott*. Do you know how hard that was? And you didn't tell me. When did you decide?"

"Cass, that's four questions. I can't keep up. I don't think I actually answered the other two yet."

She grumbled something unintelligible to him. But to his relief, she didn't pull away.

"What I said was that I *want* to stay. And the answer to your other question is yes. I *want* to kiss you." He wanted so much more than just another kiss. He wanted a lifetime with her. But if he told her now and it didn't work out...he couldn't live with that. "I don't know if it will work out for me to move back, Cass. And until I'm sure I can't promise anything."

She sniffled and slipped her arm under his elbow to wipe her nose. He hated that he'd upset her.

Fortunately, he'd turned off the main road onto the much safer lane to the bakehouse. He waited until they were in the gravel parking area where he could stop before saying more.

She pushed back from him once the buggy was parked. But rather than go to help her down, he tried to explain.

"Your *datt* said he'd give me an answer about the possibility of joining the church on Monday. Today. If the answer is positive, Cass, I promise I'll do everything I can to stay."

She paused, then looked up at him. He couldn't distinguish much of her appearance in the low light, but her voice was soft when she spoke. "Then I'll trust *Gott* with the outcome of this day."

Another similarity that grounded him. Where it mattered most, they saw eye to eye.

"*Ya*, Cass, I am, too."

Once they'd arrived at the bakehouse, Cassie's morning resembled most any work day, minus the addition of Martin. He'd pitched in and surprised her with his new knowledge of how to help in the kitchen. He'd always known as little about baking as she did about bees, but he seemed to have learned a thing or two.

Apparently, she wasn't the only one learning new things.

"Seth taught me while he was at my cabin. He's not as *goot* a cook as you, but I did eat better that week," Martin explained when she asked. And then he'd patted his stomach, as if there were actually extra pounds on his frame.

Mondays generally brought little business, unless it was a holiday weekend. She'd probably close on Mondays during the offseason. So she knew her *datt* had been up to something, when a line of local farmers had formed outside the entrance before opening.

They'd each respectfully purchased an item. And then, after the first customer had asked Martin to go outside with him, the rest had done the same. Eventually, Martin just stayed on the porch.

After an hour or more, the flow of farmers decreased. But Martin remained tight-lipped about their conversations.

By lunch, when another group of locals showed up, her patience at being left out had come to a limit. If she hadn't gotten so busy with the new stream of customers, she'd have taken a break on the porch to hear for herself. It was her bakehouse, after all.

Once she finally made change for the last order and might've finally slipped outside, she heard her *datt* and Nan's voices coming from the porch.

Ach, Nan would have the gossip sniffed out before Cassie could find out what was happening herself. And it was Cassie's business. Wasn't it?

The way Martin had talked, she'd felt as if this was about them both. But considering his exact words, maybe this didn't have anything to do with her. Maybe she just wanted to stick her nose where it didn't belong.

"Hello, Cassie." Nan entered the bakery with her usual smile and cheerful disposition.

Suddenly, Cassie saw an opportunity for a break from this tension that was about to drive her over the edge of sanity. Waiting was just the worst.

"Can you watch the store for me?" she asked Nan. But then, on second thought, there were no customers and Nan would eavesdrop on whatever was being said on the porch. Cassie took off her apron, the blue ones she'd had made especially for work in the bakeshop kitchen. "And would you mind icing some cakes?"

"Of course not. What's wrong?"

"Nothing."

"Then why are you throwing your apron at me and making a face that looks like you just ate a live toad?"

Cassie inhaled a deep breath. What had gotten into her? "*Ich bin* sorry, Nan. Would you please give me a few minutes? I just need to go for a walk to think."

"You know, I will." Nan squeezed Cassie's hand. "Take all the time you need. It's lovely out today. The fresh air will do you *goot*."

Cassie could've kissed her friend. But thoughts of kisses were putting her in a foul mood, so she banished the thought. "I'll pay you back."

"Friends don't keep tabs, silly. Go on." Nan grabbed a cinnamon bun off the shelf. "Here. This will help, too."

Martin found Cassie under a tree—not just any tree—the same one where she'd teased a swarm of bees with honey-glazed cinnamon buns. She'd given him a scare that day.

Though he knew he hadn't been nearly as frightened as she was.

He'd been growing concerned today until he found her here.

When Nan told him Cassie had gone for a walk, he hadn't imagined he'd find her so near the bees. But when all the other directions one might go for a walk had come up empty, he'd followed the old tractor trail up here to his hive yard, as a last resort.

She was sitting in the grass with her arms stretched in front of her so that her wrist came to the tops of her bent knees. Her fingers were splayed wide, and she held still, staring at them—two enchanted honeybees.

A few steps closer and he heard her laugh. Soft and bright, it carried ever so lightly on the breeze, just the same as the tickle of tiny bees' legs against the skin when they walked. He recognized the sound from his own experience.

Cassie Weaver was allowing the bees to play on her fingers. What a wonder to behold.

He hadn't known he could love her any more than he already did. His heart was already full to bursting with the news that sent him on his long search for her. Now it overflowed.

He waited, unwilling to disturb her, until she sensed him and looked across to where he stood.

"They like me." A smile teased her lips. "When I have honey on my fingers."

He imagined they'd love her no matter whether she brought honey or not. She was too lovable not to. He was drawn to her as sure as the bees were.

"You have *goot* news." She eased up from her seated position and stumbled slightly. He caught her arm and steadied her.

She latched on to his arm and didn't let go. "Will you tell me now?"

He did. He explained that he'd been given the go-ahead to be baptized and take his vows to the church this fall. And then, how Eli had gone from farm to farm, inquiring who would be willing to allow Martin to keep bees on their property.

"So that's what he was up to." Her eyes widened and her hand fluttered over her heart.

"Your *datt* must be quite a salesman, Cass. You saw them come today, one right after the other." He choked up, unable to go on. To be shown so much love was truly humbling.

She waited patiently. Funny how she had so much patience in this way and so little in others. He knew no other explanation than that *Gott* had made her for him.

"You asked me earlier when I decided to stay. I'm not sure, but I knew I had to try when I realized that I *belong* with *you*." He had to pause again when he saw her eyes well up. He was fighting tears of his own already. "You wanted me to come back because you believed that I belonged in Promise. I didn't understand how right you were about that, too—until today. It took your *datt* to show me."

Her brown eyes glistened and her lashes were wet with unshed tears, as she reached up to place a hand on each of his shoulders. "Will you kiss me now, Martin, before my heart explodes and I drown in these happy tears?"

Ya, he would. Soon. Very soon. His gaze drifted to her lips, then back to her questioning eyes. But first, he had to ask a question of his own.

He took her hands in his and kneeled before her. "Will you marry me?"

She pressed his fingers tighter in hers and bent low to kiss him on the cheek. "Silly beekeeper." Then, pulling him up to stand in front of her, she raised on her toes and kissed the other cheek. "I've waited all my life to marry you."

He embraced her and tilted his head forward so that it rested gently against her hair, then into her ear he whispered, "We belong together."

He kissed her. Their kisses were the sweetest and the best and all he'd hoped for. And he was going to keep kissing her for the rest of his days. Every. Single. One.

Chapter Eighteen

❧

Waiting until fall to marry Martin might not seem so long to everyone else, but for Cassie the weeks crept by like an eternity. She tried to take his advice about how to make time go faster by not rushing things. It didn't work.

But today he'd been baptized and taken his vows, officially joining the Amish church in Promise. At the end of the service their engagement was announced. There was nothing secret about their courtship anymore. Indeed, she had to admit their courtship had not really ever been a secret, except from the two of them.

Seth had come for the baptism, sat in the very back, then left. It was enough for Martin, who said it was likely more of a sacrifice for his prodigal brother to come than for most anyone else in attendance.

To be loved by Martin was to be loved completely. And in four weeks and two days she'd be his *frau*. The bishop insisted the wedding had to wait until after communion Sunday, which was no surprise. Yet somehow, she'd convinced her *mamm* and *datt* that she couldn't possibly wait longer than the Tuesday right after Holy Communion.

Life was going to be incredibly busy in the meantime. Her *datt* and the bishop would be visiting folks, making sure all of their members were unified before that sacred service and the foot washing that followed. All the while, she and her *mamm* would also be preparing for hundreds of guests for the wedding.

Of course, they wouldn't be alone. The entire *g'may* would rally behind them to prepare for the big event. Still, her head spun with all the work to be done. Maybe Martin was right. During this wait, time might actually go too fast for her.

Ach, nay, she could never become Martin's *frau* too soon.

"I'm sure I can guess what you're thinking about." Nan nudged her side. She and Nan were serving the sandwiches for the meal after the service. "Didn't Martin look right smart, taking his vows today?"

"*Ya*, he did." Cassie's cheeks warmed.

Nan giggled, probably quite happy to have made Cassie blush.

Only Nan would say such a thing. And for sure, only Nan could get away with a tone like that regarding Martin's looks and not offend Cassie. But there was no denying that her fiancé was *wunnerbar* handsome, especially today.

Reuben Bender passed down the line. Once he was out of hearing distance, Nan leaned over to her. "I think I should ask his forgiveness before our next communion. I should have long ago, and my conscience is not letting it go."

Cassie felt for her friend. Going to Reuben and admitting she'd wronged him would take a great deal of humility. The Lord's Supper was a holy event, and today they had been reminded of the importance of making things right, not only with *Gott*, but with one another. "I'm sure it's the right thing to do, Nan."

"*Ya*, but what if he only forgives me?"

Cassie tried to keep her voice low. "What do you mean, *only*? You've caused him a great deal of undeserved grief. And forgiveness is what you want, isn't it?"

Nan blushed a deep crimson, then pulled Cassie back from the table and lowered her voice to a whisper.

"My *datt* says we are required to forgive when one seeks forgiveness and shows a repentant spirit." Nan twisted at the ribbon on her prayer *kapp.* "But *Datt* also warned me that while Reuben may forgive me, he might not choose to trust me."

Cass wasn't about to contradict the bishop, but poor Nan. Winning Reuben's trust was likely to require a great deal of effort. "I'm sorry, Nan."

"Me, too." Her lower lip pouted. "I'll never find a match like what you have with Martin."

"*Ach,* you will, Nan. I'm sure you will."

In Cassie's current state of happiness, she could only believe that Nan would indeed find a man who loved her just for who she was.

Later that evening, the singing was held at the Burkholders' house, and Martin escorted Cassie, as he had done every church Sunday since he'd been back.

The singings in Promise were small, and once she and Martin married, the group would be smaller still.

Yet she'd enjoyed this sweet tradition while it lasted. And when it came time to go, she realized there was only to be one more in her future. After Martin helped her into the buggy and came around to the other side, she mentioned it.

"Are you glad you'll only have to endure one more of these for my sake, Martin?" She knew he wouldn't have gone if not for his wish to please her.

"Everything has its season, Cass. And I'm thankful I wasn't a *dummkopf* forever. I'd much more regret if I'd missed this special time with you." He took her hand and slipped it around his arm before he shook the reins and urged the horse into motion. "I have a little surprise for you. Would you mind a detour?"

She shook her head. "When have I ever not liked a surprise?"

He laughed. "That would be more like me, wouldn't it?"

The evenings were still long, though growing shorter. The air smelled of harvest and apples…and love. It was, after all, the season of weddings. Her heart was light and satisfied as they clipped along toward the bakehouse. But he didn't turn into the drive. Instead, he pulled up to Ada's little cottage, set the brake and turned to face her.

"I was thinking…*vell*, perhaps my *gammi* thought of it first, that this might make a perfect home for a beekeeper and the baker across the lane. Someday, I'll build you a bigger one, maybe down along Zollman's Creek when I can afford the land. But for now, *Gammi* is headed to Florida, and the cottage is ours, if you'd like it?"

Like it? *Ach*, it was a perfect little house. She'd worried about Martin's need for privacy if they lived in the bakehouse. And she'd always loved this quaint place of Ada Beiler's.

"We don't have to live here, Cass. It was only an idea. But I… I thought you might like it." Martin's forehead was creased with worry where only a minute ago he'd looked at her with such excitement.

She threw her arms around his neck and pulled him tight. "I love this house, Martin. And I love you. With all my heart, I love you and always will."

He released a long breath of relief. "I love you, too, Cass."

He stroked her hair along her temple, then traced a finger down to her ear, where he kissed her tenderly and whispered, "Forever."

* * * * *

Dear Reader,

For some years, I've hoped to write a story in which the hero or heroine has autism spectrum disorder, and I am thrilled that Love Inspired and my editor, Melissa Endlich, gave me the freedom to do so.

The weight of responsibility to do justice to Martin Beiler's character was never far from my mind. I have poured all the love an author can into creating him, as I have poured all of my mother's heart into loving and understanding this neurotypical challenge for my own son.

I hope you've enjoyed this journey back to the Amish in the beautiful highlands of Promise, Virginia. If you'd like to learn more, please visit me at amygrochowski.com.

Much Love,
Amy